Mercury HeartLink
www.heartlink.com

SCRIPTED

Thea's Tale
of Love, War and
Wisdom

SCRIPTED

Thea's Tale
of Love, War and
Wisdom

COLLEEN WALSH BREZNY

Mercury HeartLink
www.heartlink.com

Contents

PURIFICATION

LOVE

THE WORD IN MOTION

SOUNDS AND SIGHTS AND SERVANTS AND SLAVES

THE RETURN HOME

EPILOGUE

ABOUT THE AUTHOR

ACKNOWLEDGEMENTS

To Brez for being my steady listener & support as the story unfolded. Family, who will forever smile upon each other's milestones. Friends, for your infinite and sustainable presence in my life. Alison McGhee whose clear keen precise seeing birthed my writing, and whom has remained my guiding light. Margaret Nelson & Mathe Kantar for sweet encouragement. William Magdalene for beautifying my writing & believing in the essence of this work. Pam Zanetti & Pam Barnett; Stewart S. Warren & Mercury HeartLink Publishing... Woweeee!

My gratitude runs deep!

FOREWORD

Colleen Brezny is a writer of uncommon spiritual and poetic vision. I was first privileged to meet her many years ago in a classroom where her poetry delighted me with its specific, unique details. I have watched in admiration as she has grown into a writer whose work spans genres, from poetry to fiction to plays.

"Scripted," the tale of a young woman facing a journey of mythic proportions as she seeks to know her true heart, represents another stage in Colleen's growth as a writer. From the first moment I met her, I sensed in Colleen a woman whose intuitive connection to the earth and its inhabitants is stronger than that of most mortals. It is no surprise that her latest work, informed by time-honored mythology and the wisdom of the mystics, incorporates her own hard-won knowledge of what it takes to know one's own heart. It's been an honor and a privilege to witness Colleen Brezny's growth as a writer.

—Alison McGhee, Associate Professor of Creative Writing at Metropolitan State University

for
Jack & Betty & Grace
&
All peoples who brave the venture into the unfathomable,
the most precious portal of all,
The Heart.

PROLOGUE

THE FOREST: DURING A TIME ON EARTH

I am making my final preparations into what seems the abyss but in all actuality I am heading straight into the very heart of the very reason I was granted a life on earth and a precious body to carry out a mission I feel unprepared for. I am alone. My name is Thea. My parents having now gone from their respective earthly positions, harken to me a timing that has been fated for this life that I walk. I carry a faint light blue memory from old of etching my name out of sound agreeing to this mission in honor of the teachings passed forward by those who have since taken their leave of this earthly plane to whom I am grateful. And so it is...

In honor of the mission I have been provided a detailed map of the four regions that make up this forest.

The division is based on the four directions North, South, East & West. It seems death is fast approaching what was once a flourishing woods of gardens and streams and gems and critters and birds. Its inhabitants shone as stewards, regarding the life they lived amongst as crucial as the life they carried within them. Or at least, most carried within them.

There was it seems a family in the north that saw otherwise and fast created an illusion of equal concern for the life surrounding them. But unlike the purpose I am about to step into, reestablishing balance between nature and humanity based on respect and integrity.

Theirs was a mission designed solely for the family's benefit of power and wealth at all costs, even the life of the forest and all its dwellers.

Then an unfortunate fortunate event occurred, a fire raced through the North end of the forest without warning taking with it the family and nearly all family possessions except for one lone son, considered the black sheep. Left with but a few material goods this son despite the situation he now found himself in pledged to carry out the family tradition. Now he would rule. Meet Hatchet from the North, the Village of Shadows.

I study the map and learn my base is in the East Village of Skald where the sun rises and the now deserted Village of Shalimar known for its lush gardens rests in the South and finally the Village of Shayba with gems that vibrate under foot and where the sun lays its head, resides the last of the forest dwellers, it is they that have brought me here.

On this journey I am about to meet old friends, new friends and friends with wings of two sorts. Face my demons and someone else's. On this journey I will be given challenges that appear insurmountable and given lessons that turn the journey inward. On this journey I discover my weakness's and my strengths. I learn essential love and meet the "High One" I am not alone. On this journey I realize that it is everyone's journey and we are all in the forest with choices to make. On this journey I learn the freedom of forgiveness and know it to be a gift. On this journey I see the value of "Free Will" accept its proper and intended use in order to fulfill my mission. I accept this with great delight. On this journey I wish for all earthlings to recognize and value and live your purpose vs another's design for you.

Cultivate discernment and seek only the highest of truths. Question, Question, Question... and finally. On this journey I wish for you: Life in Abundance.

A Lesson in Survival

In the village of Shadows, at the North end of a great forest, lives—who many would think—an odd fellow with a rather dark sense about him. His name is Hatchet. Hatchet, it seems, is out to steal the gusto and spirit of the fairies who dwell in the village just west of the forest line. It was the mining of gemstones that brought status to Hatchet's family, who in turn enslaved, fed, clothed and controlled all forest inhabitants and the forest itself. One day a plague burned through the village killing off the entire family but Hatchet, who vows to continue the family's reign of power and wealth.

BEGINNING

Magically and without warning, where the sun rises, in the village of Skald, appears a magnificent tree house occupied by a young lady named Thea. Thea, it seems, has been given the mission to set free the inhabitants to the west. But to do so she will have to come face to face with Hatchet, and though known for her courage, she is scared.

Thea prepares for the challenge by fashioning herself a unique dress of stones, leaves and twigs. The folks in the west, whose one-time unique lifestyle has been lost to fear, now dress alike, talk alike and look alike. Upon entering the forest, Thea heads north in search of Hatchet, chanting and singing words of strength passed on by the wise and wild mothers before her.

> *The wheel of life goes round and round. The wheel of life goes round and round and we will not be bound. The wheel of life, oops! Oh oh! goes round and round and I will not be bound.*

"Oh my gosh!" thinks Thea. "Something is making me nervous round and ro...und."

Aha! rightfully so, for not far ahead Hatchet gets wind of Thea, smells trouble and begins setting up road blocks, piling footpaths with fallen trees and boulders as large as mountains, making for a treacherous hike. Just in case this is not enough, Hatchet summons Lupine, the family falcon, to buzz about Thea's head and eyes.

Exhausted from the now perilous hike and the constant ducking and swishing away of Lupine, Thea weakens and falls to the ground in a deep sleep. A sleep so profound, time goes unnoticed and day turns into night. But before long, the earth begins to rumble and

Thea, now stunned out of her sleep, hears Hatchet bellow from the North:

"You can never stop me. You are not big enough or strong enough. The empire is mine. Now leave my forest or I will have you."

Thea, now awake and trembling, sits up and begins taking slow deep breaths to center and remember herself, but still doubts her courage and mission. "Oh no," she thinks, "maybe I can't." Relying on her intuition, Thea finds her way back to the magic of her tree house.

"I could use more rest," Hatchet murmurs while preparing to head west to the village of Shayba, known for its sacred gems. "But it was well worth the effort scaring off the one who would disrupt my plan for the forest and its dwellers," he thinks.

Having now arrived unannounced in the village square, Hatchet huffs and puffs around the square like all the Hatchets before and proclaims:

"Okay, you fairies, there is trouble looming and I am warning you, it will be your demise should you be taken in by any strangers. Am I understood?"

"Yes," comes a certain voice from the crowd of villagers.

"Good, as it should be. You, I expect you to keep control of these fairies of yours."

Hatchet points to Olive, the prettiest of the fairies, whose wise eyes are but beginning to bloom. Olive speaks:

"I will, Sir."

"And remember, none of that fancy ceremony stuff. I want you digging up my gems to make yourselves worthy of eat."

"We will, Sir."

"Very well then. Let's head out, Lupine. Enough of this."

Hatchet, feeling pomp from his threats, decides to head back north for the night in hopes of a good night's rest, but not before surveying the vicinity. "I must make sure trouble will not be lurking while I am away," he thinks, then says sternly:

"Oh and by the way, just where is that Roman fellow? Not up to no good, I hope. Give him a message for me: 'Any trouble here, he pays.'"

It is Thea's friendship with Roman that has brought her back to the forest to complete a life promise of standing with each other in support of the journey. A promise made when there were no calendars. So it shall be so.

Meantime, back at the tree house, Thea restocks her supply of strength by gathering fresh feathers to place in her hair, and standing in a circle of stones beckons the trees in the forest for courage and with head held high, speaks:

"Bring me to my center, bring me to my heart! Bring me to my center, bring me to my heart!"

Then Thea confidently begins her journey through the forest to the West Village of Shayba. "Only this time," she thinks, with hope of accomplishing her mission, "I shall pass through Shalimar to the South, the village of gardens—or at least it was until the Hatchet clan drove off all the others and left the gardens to die."

It is fall and the leaves crunch as Thea descends each foot to the forest floor. To keep company along the way, she converses with the birds as they too head west. Thea senses she is being watched and stops to listen, hears loud crunching, spins around and comes Face-to-face with Hatchet, stumbles backward and is caught in the folds of an old tree where none other than Lupine sits perched just above her head. "I will play dumb," thinks Hatchet. "I will not be afraid," thinks Thea. Hachet says:

"Pardon me. Might you be heading to Shalimar? I am ahead of myself. First let me tell you who I am. I am the last reigning member of the Hatchet clan, infamous for our watch over the forest, as I am out and about doing today. Now where might you be heading? And what did you say your name was?"

"Well, Sir, my name, Sir, is Thea and I have heard of your beautiful gardens in Shalimar to the South and desired the sight of them for myself.... It is foretold the scent of the blossoms renews the spirit and so is well worth any peril one might encounter in a forest as deep as this...."

At which point Lupine begins to squawk, flutters from tree to tree, just missing Thea, only to land at her boots, kick up dirt, and be reproached by Hatchet:

"Whatever are you doing? Excuse me, Thea. Meet Lupine, my trusted servant. She is simply saying hello and means no harm."

"Oh really!" thinks Thea, who nods to Lupine and inquires:

"I hear tell of a warm spring and waterfall, should I need water upon my arrival to Shalimar."

"That is quite true."

"Well then, I will continue on before the sun goes below the horizon. Good to have greeted you" (secretly relieved to be on her way).

"Oh! But before you go, just what is your purpose in my forest?

"Just the gardens, Sir."

"So your stay is short?"

"Why yes, unless of course I feel called to move about before journey's end."

So the two part ways believing they have each cleverly baffled the other with their intentions. Not for long. Lupine has been sent to follow Thea at a safe distance and spy on her position and motives.

Thea stops to sing and chant, asking the wise ones for guidance and instruction, and for strength to meet her mission—saving the fairies and the livelihood of the forest. "I must reach my destination and accomplish my purpose," she thinks, "without a threat from that old buzzard from the north, but oh how I think that is not going to happen!"

In the west, Olive and the other fairies are in great distress as food and fresh water are no longer plentiful. A dark worry has settled over the village, whose gaiety has long sense disappeared. On this day, Olive will slip away at dusk to gather herself in a nearby grove of aspens, which for some peculiar reason revive the weary of heart when entered in silence. Not this night—Olive returns to the village more worried than ever. She cries:

"I have lost my hope and the beat of my heart has slowed—whatever will we do?"

"My heart is breaking," laments Thea, "and my legs feel like lead. I must create my circle and rest in it if I am to go on." When out of the blue, Lupine dashes up from behind and swipes a wing alongside Thea's head, knocking her to the ground and out cold. Only one more right turn and Thea would be in what is now the wasteland of Shalimar and its infamous gardens.

Now, on Lupine's return to Hatchet, Thea whirls deep into a dream, a dream of knowledge, and finds herself in the original Shalimar, standing in one of its many gardens. She whispers:

"Oh my, what beauty!"

Spotting a fountain whose water runs cool to the touch, she stops to freshen her face, then heads toward a grove of pear trees, whose juice—perfectly sweet—lightens her mind. "To bathe would be a blessing, so I will wander 'til I hear the stream," she thinks. As she heads in the direction of the Sun, time slows itself, and magically Thea is swarmed in the breaths of butterflies and dragonflies, leading her to somewhere other than the stream, which she can now hear. She wonders aloud: "Where am I headed?! Oh, dear. What must become of me? Just how much faith is one to have?"

A voice says:

"The answer, dear one, is: no more than you already have. You must simply remember it, and who you are."

Thea turns in the direction of the voice and sees in front of her two figures sitting on a bench, smiling and motioning for her to come near.

"Fear not, Thea. We are here now, always have been and always will be. This, Thea, is your first lesson: to trust—to trust that you are not alone and that you have within you what is required to meet your task on earth. Before we get started, let us introduce ourselves. I, Thea, am Rose."

Then comes a boom of a voice:

"I, Thea, am Justice."

Thea begins to doubt, pray and wonder—all at once—about what to say to what is before her eyes, when Justice speaks:

"I see you are in doubt of the truth of our beingness, but that is common. Most earthlings doubt anything that is not physical. That is why we felt it best to physically present ourselves to you—to begin to alleviate your doubt. Though only on occasion physically present, we are forever near. We are watching over you, and all you need do is call upon us..."

Rose says:

"So, Thea, let us begin. Listen deeply, Thea. Listen to the silence and I assure you that you will carry in your body the energy of the lesson. You were born with strengths and weaknesses. It is the gift of your strengths that will support the learning necessary to becoming authentic. Though you believe yourself not to be, you are brave. Your challenges will prove it to you."

Justice speaks:

"You have been provided everything you would ever need within your own unique map of constellations, like a fingerprint but in the sky. Like you, we are of God."

Rose speaks:

"Don't bother looking outside yourself. It is but a distraction and a detour, though you are welcome to take it. However, be forewarned: oneself ultimately cannot be avoided.......... The fear is of death, physical death, but your will to survive is most potent and provides your heart with courage. Thea, the seeds we are planting will come into bloom over time. Your task is to care for your body with tenderness and kindness in order to receive your spirit. You must be grounded or you will flounder and suffer and yield no crop."

Justice speaks:

"Before we take our leave, let us request guidance and blessings upon each of us, and may we step out in our correct place, poised to move forward in grace. Truly!"

And poof, they are gone, or at least gone from sight. "Oh my gosh!" thinks Thea, "What, pray tell, have I gotten myself into? I must rest. Or have I been resting? I think I was about to bathe.

Slipping into the streams cool water, Thea's mind quiets, a warmth of heart emanates outward and her body, now engulfed, takes up earth to complete her restoration... "My mind is still, my heart is open, my body is grounded." To counter the fear still whistling through her senses, Thea softly chants over and over:

"Bring me to my center, bring me to my heart!"
Remembering her journal, Thea decides to record the events of the
last few days, but before doing so, she reads the inscription from
her grandmother Grace:

- to my darling granddaughter - my bright eyed one -
whose heart sees all - endowed with this gift of sight
whose weight is cumbersome.

- gift with burden - lean, dear one, into the giver and
not the gift nor the burden and you will master - your
essence - I am with you.....

Thea now dried and warmed by the sun enters a last thought in
her Journal. "I have," she writes, "a will divine for my use, and
value equal to that of all others. I have life in me for good, from the
source of one heart. I will learn a love without conditions." Placing
her journal in a safe place, Thea dresses and forgets not to secure
twigs and bones in her hair, plucks two pears from a tree, makes
a reverent bow to the gifts given and received while in Shalimar,
and heads west.

FARCE OF A FEAST

To the North, Hatchet, along with his sidekick Lupine, is brewing up a storm. Plotting they are a devious act and dressing it up to appear charitable and kindly. Hatchet snaps:

"Lupine, we've got to get ahead of this girl; we are going to seduce away any confidence she may harvest, along with herself proclaimed God-given mission."

Lupine, hearing it all before, lazily spreads her wings and spurs a caw to appear enthused. Hatchet barks:

"Now, are you with me Lupine? Awfully quiet today. So bird, speak up!"

"Caw, caw, caw!"

"That's better. I will be in need of your keen eyes and wing speed, but for now we make a plan." "I say we invite her to spend the night and dine with us, insisting that the weather has turned inclement and far too dangerous for a girl to travel alone."

"Well, Lupine, I must say, for a bird I think you are on to something. While she is in our midst we will convince her of our goodness and sincerity regarding her well-being. So let us get about gathering and preparing a feast fit for a queen—or rather a king. But we must clean this place, it is a mess. Ta, ta, Lupine, get about the work."

"So, Master, how will we know where she is?"

"Just go about your business, Lupine, and leave that to me."

In the meantime, Thea, traveling through the forest, is sensing that old familiar doubt and fear. Spying a rather large stone ahead and to her left, she decides to sit a bit and listen deeply for any help that might be trying to get her attention. "I do fear I could drowned in this fear and doubt that I seem so plagued with," she thinks. "I must quiet this mind of its sorrow—or is it my heart?" Thea wonders aloud:

"Where is it that peace comes from?"

Suddenly, leaves of orange, reds and yellows slowly swirl their way to the ground, piling up at Thea's feet. Paying no attention, she shouts to the sky:

"Just what do you want from me? I am not enough for this journey."

Then it occurs to her she ought to chant her prayer:

"Bring me to my center, bring me to my heart! Bring me to my center, bring me to my heart!"

As the leaves continue to fall, a rather rambunctious herd of wild turkeys with poults arrives. Thea, taking notice, observes the hens teaching their poults to forage for food, as the hens maintain a motherly eye. Thea is momentarily distracted as the leaves—it seems—begin to dance, spiraling into the air, making music as they tumble into each other's dry edges, then quietly settling to the ground. There stands Rose. In awe and tears, Thea approaches the wise one. Rose says:

"You called, Thea, and here I am. What can I do for you, my dear? Speak your heart. It will show me how to best guide you."

"My heart, it seems, is heavy with fear and doubt in my ability to fulfill a purpose that appears much bigger than I am prepared to handle."

"Answer me this, Thea. Is it your heart or your mind that is gripped by doubt and fear?"

"Oh, Rose, you must know it is my mind, and then my heart knows not what to do."

"That being the case, Thea, let us begin your next lesson: First your listening must be from a place deep within. To listen with your mind alone will only get you so far, and barely near where you need to go. Do you understand?"

"Yes, I believe I do." Thea nods.

"So let us proceed. This fear that grips you, it is a force that delights on darkness, Thea, and your purpose is to bring light to this world of yours. So can you see how it is that you are a threat?"

"I guess so. Yet I feel threatened and incapable of this task. So, you see, it is hard to think of myself as a threat to anyone or anything."

"I know, dear. However, that is your doubt and fear speaking. It is your darkness...and yours to master if you will lead others. Did you notice the attentive eye the mother turkeys kept on their poults?"

"Yes!"

"Did you notice that as attentive and watchful as those bird mothers were, they allowed their babies freedom to move about with their natural scratching and hunting and pecking, and even squabbling? You see, Thea, this must be the position you create regarding those very powerful feelings and emotions that stop you flat in your tracks—unlike those turkeys, which move with purpose—to survive. For, Thea, you must master the art of having your emotions but not being them, denying them or judging them. In order to thrive and fulfill your intended destiny, discover what you love and what you are passionate about. This knowledge will prove to be key. Nor must you mistake others' emotions for your own. To stay in harmony, Thea, you need a broader perspective than what emotions alone can provide. While the turkeys need only to look down at the ground for what they need to stay alive, you must look up and around. Finally, Thea, to delight in your life with passion and love is how you fight that which would otherwise take you down. Our lesson is complete, and I am about to depart. Let the lesson seep into you, Thea. You are blessed by the force that surrounds you. Lean into it."

A swoosh, as the leaves once again stir in a whirl. Thea, alone, stands silently in awe before moving on. With Roman, Olive and the West Village heavy on her heart, determination is fast becoming a momentous inspiration.

LEFT IN THE WINDS OF DECEPTION, DOUBT BUILDS A NEST ON A BROKEN LIMB

Hatchet mutters:

"If I were a praying sort of guy, right about now I'd be on my knees. But, Lupine, planning, planning! That's what I am about. I am not about to lose control. Lupine, please stop scratching in the dirt. It makes me nervous. Besides, is all the food gathered for the feast of kings?"

Lupine spits and sputters a bird "yes," knowing what is to come down the pike. Hatchet shouts: "Well then, wood, wood! We need a lot of wood, so off with you. I will join you in a flash. First I must put the final touches on the plot to distract, confuse and throw doubt into this troublemaker."

"I am becoming weary of all this nonsense," thinks Pastoral Langely Hatchet. "That is the first time I have thought of my name in a long time. Now, where is that bird when I need him?" Hatchet mumbles:

"How on earth could they have named me Pastoral Langely? What were they thinking? I showed them. Hasn't bothered me in years. Now where is that bird anyway? The next thing is to find out where that little missy is on her march through my forest. That bird, where on earth..."

When all of a sudden, landing at Hatchet's feet is Lupine. Hatchet says:

"So, my trusted servant, it is getting about time we send you out to spy on the whereabouts of our unsuspecting guest. I will need a full report on any suspicious meandering or...or if there are others with her that could botch our plan. So, off with you."

Sputtering under her breath—as only a bird can do—about her horrible treatment, Lupine sends out a defiant "caw!" Hatchet barks:

"Well, bird, just what would you have me do? You are lucky I haven't eaten you. Where is my iron kettle?"

Lupine, smarter than one would imagine, calmly walks near the lean-to, points a sharp right wing in the kettle's direction, lifts in the air and is gone from sight.

The Mind's Doubt Is the Heart's Loss

Reenergized after her lesson with Rose regarding her emotions and their affect on outcome, Thea is determined to not allow her fear, her anger or her doubt debacle her destiny as bringer hope to her friends in the west. Unaware of being spied on from overhead, she decides to take a short time for silence and prayer, and begins to arrange an area to lay out her stones, beads and—most precious of all—her journal. Thea prays:

"My prayer this day to you, oh source of life, would be for the courage not to succumb to my fear. In turn, I offer you this most sincere chant, from my heart to yours and the hearts of those whose guidance I could not do without."

With hands high to the sky, Thea makes a bow, walks three times in a circle, then enters the circle's center to begin her prayerful chant:

"Bring me to my center, bring me to my heart!
Bring me to my center, bring me to my heart!"

Taking a last slow turn around the circle's rim as a final blessing, Thea gives thanks:

"To the wise ones who are guiding me, be you in spirit or physical form, I make an offering of gratitude through this song in my heart."

And a song of love's yearning fills the forest. Appearing at the forest's edge are a deer, a fox and a wolf.

Lupine's feathers fluff with excitement, and she nearly falls from the limb she is perched on. "Just wait till I return with the news of others," she thinks, and off she goes, forgetting in her excitement to make note of Thea's location and to determine the distance she must travel before approaching the Hatchet camp to the North.

As if in slow motion, Thea gathers her precious treasures and returns the journal to her pouch after recording the healing prayer. She pulls out her compass, nourishes herself on a pear, stands erect and humbly embarks onward toward her destiny. With Roman and the others pressing on her heart, Thea catches a glimpse in her mind's eye of what appears to be a solemn camp of kindred spirits. She scans for Roman. He senses her, and with that, each are comforted with the mission before them.

Sputtering and crashing into camp, kicking dust up everywhere,

Lupine falls over, picks her bird-self up and begins to caw for Hatchet, who is nowhere in sight. Hearing muffled sounds, Lupine heads carefully in their direction and to her amazement finds Hatchet, who appears to have been crying. No sooner does Hatchet spy Lupine, when he jumps to his feet and starts in on the bird:

"Okay, Lupine," starts Hatchet whose eyes it seem are now bulging out of their sockets. Lupine, getting nervous, begins to tell the tale of the others and the odd meanderings of the girl. All the while, the "girl" is inching closer to an invitation she never saw coming.

DIM ON HOPE

The seams are severely fraying in the usually very peaceful village in the West. Its folks are fast running out of patience with their predicament and with one another. Roman speaks:

"Olive, may I rely on you?"

"Why, yes. What is it I might do?"

"I need you to calm the women and the children before things get any more out of hand. I will see what I can do with the men. What has been hidden in each of us, Olive, has come to the surface under all the stress, and it is not a pretty picture. We must learn and teach simultaneously. So let us get busy."

And the two set about understanding an invitation of another kind—a test of their hearts.

Hatchet speaks:

"So how far away would be your measurement before the girl gets to us?"

Lupine hears the question and her feathers began to visibly shake, for she does not know and that was an important point of the secret flyby. So, sputtering and stuttering, the bird instead looks straight into Hatchet's bulging eyes and says:

"I do not know. The scene was so astonishing, in my excitement it did not occur to me to count air time."

"Well, well, well. It seems you brought back some of the girl's attitude, however. Let's see. What shall we do? I know! Go back without a moment's waste, for we have a dinner to prepare and a table to don with our best."

"We do not have a best," thinks Lupine, who then kicks up dust and lifts off.

With Lupine off the grounds, Hatchet prepares—in his fury—a dubious hoax to regain control of the situation and squash any attitude that the bird may be taking up with. Hatchet thinks aloud:

"Aha, I will build a birdcage and cage the little devil for three days, feed him not a morsel nor a drop of water."

So Hatchet busies himself while awaiting the bird's return.

Through the forest flies Lupine. She spots the girl flitting down an old path—untraversed in what appears a century—happily as if she had just been crowned queen for a day. Without notice of the spy, Thea recites to herself a favorite poem:

> *The sun shone on me*
> *While its wind took my breath gone*
> *Pressed me to the earth alive*
> *Setting again west*

When all of a sudden, a bird falls from the sky. For it seems Lupine was stung by a wasp and caught off guard. Down the bird goes and lands right at Thea's feet. Startled but for a moment, Thea inquires:

"Hmmmm, now don't I know you? Of course! You are the falcon Lupine."

Feeling a bit foolish as a fallen falcon, Lupine brushes it all off but is secretly attracted to Thea's concern about her well-being.

"I am fine, girl, but I must get about my day," says Lupine shyly. No sooner is she there, she is gone.

Flying at high speed, Lupine wings it back to the North camp to deliver her red squirrel meat and notices Hatchet busily setting a table fit for nobility. Puzzled at finding the old hoot doing anything without that report as to the girl's distance by foot. With a crash landing, Lupine enters camp to the smells of roasted brambles. She wonders what else is a brew. Hatchet says: "So, upon your second return do you bring me the news I am in need of, bird?"

Cawing out a nervous yes to her master, Lupine makes it utterly clear the girl ought to arrive in camp in two hours. Hatchet says:

"I will need your assistance in gathering the ingredients to fill out the menu. When that is finished, we will have a lesson."

"A lesson," thinks the bird. "Aha, that's the other stew I smelled brewin' on my landing."

"This is what you are to gather: moss for soup, mushrooms and pine nuts for salad, elderberries for tea, and, finally, boughs of green for decor. While you are off doing that, I will hang the lanterns in the trees to view our evening by. Oh, and return swiftly for your lesson."

The silly bird has no clue what's coming down the pike.

One hour later, not only are the lanterns hung but so is the birdcage. Dragging a stuffed burlap sack of the feast's menu behind him, Lupine returns looking nervous and exhausted. Hatchet shouts:

"Drop it where you be, old bird. Our time is brief and the lesson is utmost."

Just as Lupine is freeing herself from the bag of morsels, Hatchet grabs her from behind and quickly hoists her into the birdcage and secures the door. Lupine, who barely gets a caw out, finds herself imprisoned. Hatchet spits:

"That, my bird, is for not listening to or executing my demands while under threat in my forest. Now that you're in the cage, I am left to finish the feast myself and to deal with this snip of a girl on my own. You'd better hope I get the job done, or those wings of yours will see the sky no more."

The stunned bird is so at a loss she blanks out her own song, and a call for help seems unlikely.

False Pride Is the Mask Purchased by Illusion

Meanwhile Thea, believing she is on a roll after her lesson and feeling a bit invincible, trips on a rock in the middle of the path and takes a tumble hard enough to throw her off kilter, which sets her cycle of self doubt back into motion. "O mother god, here I am again on my knees after thinking I had finally figured it out," she thinks. A voice in her head proclaims:

"Oh, Thea, you have not been listening."

"It must be Rose speaking."

"No, Thea, this is your grandmother Grace. How are you sweet darling?"

"Well, grandmother, if I can get up from the ground and dust off I will better know," says an embarrassed Thea.

"No, my little darling. How are you inside, Thea? Inside your head, inside your heart, dear one?"

And a weeping Thea sits upon the earth, despairing of her loneliness and aloneness. ‹time lapse›

"Go ahead and weep, Thea. I am with you in your sorrow."

"But grandmother, it was only minutes ago that I was singing. How must I ever understand the ways of my being? How, grandmother?"

"The journey of your undertaking is a mighty one consisting of everything, my precious."

"Grandmother I want you here," Thea cries.

"Oh, my precious jewel, I too struggled as a young woman. All humans do. In that, you are not alone. Let me remind you of your lesson with Rose, the one regarding your emotions. Though you have emotions, you are not your emotions. Remember that? Emotions are the language of the body, and one's relationship to those emotions plays an important role in the quality of a life. Do you understand?"

"Well, what do you mean, a relationship with emotions?"

"Listen, child, we must get you grounded. Did you trip over a rock, Thea, or might it have been a lie? When we stand in the truth, only then are we grounded. What tripped you up was a lie, Thea. You must name it and turn the stone over to get to the truth. Let your emotions become a bell ringing, alerting you to probe for a greater realization of yourself, another, or a situation. That's the relationship you want to nurture."

"Grandmother, I masked my insecurity and fear in arrogance. That is my lie."

"My darling, in all truth there are more lies. Feel, Thea, the shawl of love I have wrapped you in. This, my dear one, is your barometer."

"What, grandmother?"

"The feeling, Thea, the difference between a truth and a lie. Ponder now what I have just given you. Make it yours, Thea, not only something I simply told you. With that accomplished you will have embodied the lesson, making you a candidate for mastery. Time is the gift."

"I love you, grandma."

"My love is all yours. I will be just around the corner."

"Oh, grandma!"

As Thea hoists herself off the ground, a song long forgotten sings itself in her heart. And in the atmosphere an echo, "Remember your roots, remember your roots, remember your roots...." "I will catch up with the song later," thinks Thea. "Now, instead, I will silence my mind to send love to the West Village." A nagging feeling regarding the lie she uncovered during her lesson haunts her. "I am hungry and tired," thinks Thea, "and the sun will retreat soon."

GEMS STREWN UPON THE PATH

Hatchet shouts:

"He l l o o o ! He l l o o o ! Is that you girl? Are you out there?"

Thea, nervous, stops to listen. Again he shouts:

"He l l o o o !"

"Oh my, ought I respond or simply ignore and move faster?" wonders Thea. "Am I really a spark of light?" Before it is clear what to do, Thea and Hatchet are staring at each other. He speaks:

"Well, girl, my bird reported your whereabouts in my forest and out of concern I've come searching for you. It seems we are in for some mighty nasty weather and I thought it best you veer to the north for shelter from the storm. Ever see a forest storm, girl? More dangerous than one would guess."

"My name is Thea."

"Oh—pardon me, pardon me. Can I convince you to come north with me for shelter from the storm?"

"There doesn't seem to be a cloud in the sky, Sir. From what might I be sheltering? With limited time for exploring your lovely forest, it would be unwise to waste it," says Thea with confidence.

"The storm is coming out of the west and will be upon us within a matter of a few short hours, so it seems the only logical course would be to shelter in the north with the bird and me, where provisions for one's comfort are plentiful."

Cautiously Thea agrees:

"All right then, but upon its passing I will make swift my leave to appease my sojourn."

"Remember your roots, remember your roots," are the next words Thea hears. Turning north, the oddest of pairs heads to shelter from of a storm all right. Just not the one Thea was anticipating. Thea asks:

"Are you concerned at all for the West Villagers?"

"Oh the West Villagers, my fondest of neighbors, have weathered all weathers with the same ease upon which they arrive and depart. So you need not worry yourself girl."

Well, upon hearing this, suspicion creeps into Thea's mind. "If the weather can be managed with ease by the West," she thinks, "can it really be that menacing? It is true that out here I have no cover. I could high foot it back to my tree house for shelter, but how far away might it be? It is his tone of voice I am wary of." Growing irritated, she says:

"My name is Thea."

"Don't get so touchy, girl. A little gratitude for my virtuous consideration, Miss Thea, is what is called for in this situation."

An uncomfortable silence settles over them as they head north. "I've got her where I want her," thinks Hatchet. "I must stay centered and remember my roots," thinks Thea, who silently calls upon Justice's direct guidance. Remembering the song placed long ago in her heart, Thea sings:

> True I sing to you of something true there is a peace in all hearts
> there is a peace in all hearts I sing to you of something true
>
> A peace that shan't depart A peace that shan't depart I sing to
> you of something true

Suddenly, Justice beams in and counsels Thea to observe and witness with all her senses Hatchet's words and behaviors and—just as importantly—what he is not saying. After a long silence, Hatchet under his breath begins to mumble and rant. Thea cannot make out his rant. She asks:

"Are you saying something to me?"

"No, no I am not," Hatchet mutters.

"I am wondering, Sir, just how long before we arrive at the North Village?"

"It is hard to say. If all goes well, in time for a warm meal."

Resuming her singing to distract, Hatchet begins getting annoyed with what he deems as frivolity, and resumes chattering under his breath. Then a peculiar thing occurs. A hawk whirls straight from the heavens, landing on the path in front of Thea. Then another peculiar occurrence—in the next moment, the path becomes life threateningly treacherous. Moss-blackened boulders freeze Thea in her tracks as Hatchet stumbles to the ground with a quakerous thud. He shouts:

"Well isn't this just a fine thing you have gotten me into."

Hatchet rolls and spews and spits in an effort to get himself off the ground. Thea offers him her hand, which he takes—though he greatly despises it because he feels a fool—and with all her might gets the old hoot upright, and there leaves to him to finish.

A War Between Minds

In a steaming huff, Thea stomps her foot on the ground—all the while putting her sticks and bones back in her hair, which appears but wild fury on her head—and proclaims, shouting:

"Listen, you old man, if you think for one minute you are going to speak to me in a dissenting tone, clearly you are in denial of my determination to carry on with my purpose in this world. I'd prefer death by forest storm any day to taking refuge in your camp. I am not the cause of your predicament. Someone else planted those dark seeds in you."

"Oh yeah, girl, and who planted yours in you? Seems all those prayers you heard chantin' around here ain't workin' too well, are they?"

"My prayers are working just fine, old man."

At that remark, the hawk decides to fly over Hatchets head, and hovers but for a moment. Thea makes a discreet chuckle as Hatchet touches the mess on top his head, and all heck breaks out. The cussing seems to go on for as long as honey is slow to pour.

#*^!-_+*^##-!-‹›?@%!!!*, and *_++‹›#@%! **, and ^_+$#@!!%*)-

Thea, sensing the standstill between them, sits on a boulder to rest her now weary, drained self as Hatchet jerks clumsily vertical, grabs a handful of foliage from a nearby clump of weeds, and scours his head and hands. Hearing her name echo as if in a canyon, Thea stills her mind to see, standing there in dead silence, Rose, Justice, and Grace, but in that silence they fade out, leaving Thea to recollect her lessons: "Remember your roots! I am so frustrated in this very moment at the injustice going on here, I really don't care right now about being all wise. Grace speaks:

"Is this, Thea, the performance of a child raised with sight fashioned for a purpose?"

"Grandmother, maybe it is just more than I can bear."

"Maybe not, dear one. I am off."

"Why must I be alone?"

Silence.

Hatchet speaks:

"So, Princess Thea!"

"What do you mean 'so'? If I recall, it was you who felt it necessary to seek out my presence. Besides, I see not a cloud."

"Oh you will."

"I fully intend to maneuver the boulders carefully. To be reckless will but assure sloppiness, which is certain to delay our arrival to safety from the storm that I simply do not see."

Defying Thea's slow going notion, Hatchet whisks by like an arrow let loose from its bow, on its way to take dinner. Thea, on the other hand, expels a sigh of disgust at the scene and finds her mind back in a world of turmoil. She says to the wind:

"Gee, for a moment I thought there was a God."

In the next moment, Thea finds herself sitting on a throne in dialogue with an invisible conversant which goes something like this:

"Okay, wise one, why am I here?"

"You, Thea, came seeking me. By all means, proceed at your delight."

"Well, the results of all my efforts for God just don't seem to be paying off—I pray, I chant, I dance, I sit silent, I sing, I recite sacred poetry. The birds and I love each other. I care for others and myself. I believe in justice and truth. Yet I am rattling in frustration. why am I here, wise one, on earth I mean? While the cruel and wicked, the sellers of tainted diamonds, have silenced the humble with fear, voicing verse upon verse of their making, maintaining the diamond collection and skating merrily across the earth."

"Well, quite a mouthful, but we take pleasure in a lass as sassy as you. Maybe a breath or two to quiet that charming mind. What of the notion of listening? Might that appeal to you or not? It appears you swing on a vine between hope and hopelessness, while neither is grounded in absolute truth, be it worldly or otherworldly. We have noticed that you and those like you with bodies do want to believe you are in control. Yes, Thea, even you. It is but fear clothed in stiff cloth. This we do not pleasure in. Our delight is to extinguish your anguish."

"I do not understand these ideas you speak of."

"I am but planting seeds, Thea. In time, their meaning will be revealed."

Suddenly, Thea finds herself stuck between two boulders, having no clue how but quite stunned at her situation. With but a vague and hazy recollection of the experience just prior, she decides she is in need of assistance and hollers:

"Hey! Hey! Hey!"

"I so don't want to ask that old hoot for help," she thinks. There he stands, saying:

"Need a hand up girl?"

"Yes, yes I do, if you would be so kind."

Slightly dizzied from the tumble, the two continue the journey north in silence, each mulling over the odd and mystifying events of the day—Thea's invisible conversation and Hatchet's humiliating experience when the hawk deposited on his head.

The Revelation

The scent of a roasting dinner breaks the dark silence between the ravished travelers when Hatchet proclaims:

"Just around the bend and we have arrived."

More bothered than ever by the lack of weather, Thea offers up a word of thanks for the hospitality:

"I am grateful for the concern, for by now, hunger and exhaustion have quelled all other sensations."

As they turn the bend, a table fit for the finest is in bird's eye view, and for a moment the worry of storm loses its immediacy.

"Caw, caw, caw! Caw, caw, caw! Caw, caw, caw!" screams Lupine from overhead, suffering from caged punishment. "Shush up old bird, things are just fine." pleads Hatchet in an attempt to create an illusion of normalcy. Suddenly, over head screeches the hawk, flips the cage setting free the Falcon.

"That blasted fiend "shouts Hatchet. With an edge, Thea inquires:

"Just what is going on here?"

"There is no weather, is there now? You brought me here under false pretenses to wrinkle up my purpose. Well, let me assure you of this, you old hoot, never!"

"I will set my own trap," she thinks, "and I will worry not of the birds. For the moment, they are free. It is my freedom I must secure." She requests: "So, I am famished and in much need of a feast of such work. Would hate to see it go to waste. May I?"

Touched at the twist of things, Hatchet solemnly satisfies Thea's bold request. She says:

"The caging of Lupine was—for what now?"

"Lupine was being taught a lesson. It is how things are done in the north. It is our way. We shall sit now at the table. Guests first."

THE FEAST BEGINS

Upon lifting the first spoonful, a silent "thank you" from Thea and the chatting begins. Thea digs:

"It seems 'Hatchet' would be an odd title. Do you like it? and is it the name you were bequeathed with?"

A pause of some duration inclines Thea to believe she may have hit on something, something weighing heavily on one's heart. With head down and voice wobbling, Hatchet speaks:

"Pastoral Langely. How would anyone take to being called Pastoral Langely? Well, well, it just wasn't going to work for me."

"So naming yourself Hatchet does what? Make you feel strong, in control, manly, in a way that Langely did not?"

Pause. Hatchet, with arms folded leans back on his stool sends a glare of disgust in Thea's direction, and proclaims:

"If you think, Miss. Thea, your conspicuous concern will jostle me from my position over the forest, you have misread the signs. There is no threat to my ownership of the gems, the brooks and the gardens, and of all the lowly creatures who inhabit here. This, girl, is my domain. What pray tell does it matter? You are here but out of curiosity."

"Sorry to have offended one in one's home, so generous with nourishment. It's just that I could have sworn I felt a broken heart," says a calm Thea. Then Lupine crashes the party, upturning Hatchet, his stool and the entire feast with table. Thea goes unscathed, while Hatchet lies there nearly in tears though shouting profanities at both Lupine and Thea, none of which can be understood, with one exception:
"Get out of my forest, girl. You are a bad omen here. There has been nothing but trouble since your arrival. Do not let me see you

creeping in my vicinity again. There is no need for you. Do you hear me?"

"You, Mister Hatchet, are nothing but phony. You have no time for the truth because it will spoil your conjured up web of false control of everything, when in fact you have control of nothing, Pastoral Langely. I see through you. I am happy to leave. You are poison with that attitude. But let me tell you this—this contrived mess you have yourself in is the poison. You threw away your real self for a false self, Pastoral Langely. I dare you to make peace. Farewell!"

Thea stomps off, leaving Hatchet in the dust. The falcon and the hawk lead Thea back east to replenish and remember.

PURIFICATION

"I feel better simply facing east. I shall take the path a bit before I stop to better myself," Thea tells herself with a sigh of relief. However, in no time Thea's fear is making it difficult for her to put one foot in front of the other. Spying a lone boulder, she decides to collect herself and sets about to journal. Oh! When low and behold, who should appear but none other than the "Trio," Grace, Rose, and Justice.

"Looks to us it is time for another lesson. Would you agree, dear one?"

"I do, grandmother. I am so frightened, and I no longer recall what it is that frightens me."

"Might it be of your own self, my dear?"

"Not only of my own self but even of that higher force you speak of, grandmother."

"Your frights, dear one, are not uncommon. We mortals seem beset with this burden. Let us chat later on this. More pressing is the gift Justice brings to you this day, Thea, my grace I leave you," whispers Grace.

JUSTICE FOR JUSTICE AND ROSE IN HAND

Thea, humming with nervousness in anticipation for the arrival of Justice, is left waiting and waiting and waiting, up to the edge of fuming. Justice exhorts:

"Thea!"

"Yes," Thea replies, startled.

"The waiting, Thea, was part of the lesson, to begin to show you parts of yourself that are the cause of your troubles. Do you understand?"

"Because I was angered?" asks a sheepish Thea.

"Thea, what you and your people must come to understand is this: Number one—what lie deep inside must be rendered to the light of day, for it will certainly take down even the best of us. It is referred to as one's 'Shadow.' At the center of it, lies a jewel. Number two

—how you use the gift of 'life Force' is a choice minute by minute, requiring attention, focus, presence, diligence, thoughtfulness and consideration. For what comes from you moves out into the world to all of humanity. The quality of one's force is determined by the beliefs held inside the mind and the heart. Number three— to grow in the understanding of one's self and its relationship to others and to the universe, the planet and where we originated from is our journey. It provides, a map, a focus, a correct intention. All of this is within. When you are correct with you, you will be correct with the rest. So, Thea, as you continue east ask of yourself the tough questions. Perhaps—what do you have in common with Hatchet? Is he not a mirror? And where is it you have placed your trust, in fear or in the force? What has made you a victim? Do you respect the use of your will?"

Rose speaks:

"Thea, it is Rose. To journey with the thorns, I bring you the gift of compassion, for it will make possible the seemingly impossible. Our love we leave you."

"Oh my," ponders Thea. "I am not certain I know of what he speaks. I am not like Hatchet. How could I be? I suppose I have a temper, but who wouldn't with all the injustice going on in this forest." Deciding to record in her journal the lesson Justice laid out, Thea begins to sense that she is not alone. With a shiver running up her spine and a cold northerly wind upturning, a blanket of ice quite magically covers the forest that surrounds her. "Well fancy that, I thought it would be easy making my way east."

The Burrowing Begins in Earnest

"Bring me to my center, bring me to my heart," mumbles Thea and a great sleep takes over, accompanied by a dream of death. The hawk and falcon hover over head as each comes and goes from the dream, knowing the risks of purifying. This is what Thea observes.

The Dream

Under bright lights, dressed in luminous colors, at a square table sits a figure like that of a schoolmarm, hurling questions at Thea, with a rather large ticking clock nearby, signaling quickened responses required. Each timed question pops out of a black box of which there are 1,000.

"So Ms. Thea, how does your anger serve you?"

"Well it, it makes me feel strong, but it does not seem to be working anymore. I am angry at betrayal, I thought life was loving."

Next: "And what is your sorrow?" A weeping Thea drops chin to chest beseeching the loneliness that lives in her heart.

Next: "And to what do you give to fear?"

"I give away my soul." At this Thea observes a rectangular table behind the marm, carrying upon its sparkling polished top, in every color of the spectrum, a gem in geometric form. She wonders of this, but there is little time for wonder. The black boxes are popping one after another. The clock's hands have now fallen off and have been replaced by a giant hour glass, and Thea is dimming. "So this is purification," she thinks. Finally the last box, its question asked very slowly:

"So, Thea, tell me, do you love Thea?"

"No, we are taught to not," Thea replies proudly.

"It is no wonder you have been sent to this school. Your guidance is highly misdirected. Your lesson, dear young woman, is to love Thea. We are through."

Then out a window appears the ocean, upon which the 1,000 black boxes burn with a flame as orange as a setting sun. When suddenly, in a roofless room a round and gilded table is prepared and Thea takes her place. Next: floating servants bring forward each handpicked gem, Thea's natural gifts long forgotten. Then the ever flowing grace appears.

"I did say I would get back to you. These gifts, Thea, are your strengths—where the genuine Thea resides. Your ability to use 'the will' as intended is now aligned with 'the high one.' We bid you the fruit of your labor."

A Nudge to Waken

A rustling Thea is awakened by a soft breeze to both cheeks fanned by the wings of Hawk and Falcon. "Oh my," ponders a still Thea. "The High One." Realizing that her dream of counsel might vanish from memory, Thea logs it into her journal but finds herself most curious of "The High One," remembering too her instruction to examine her ways like those of Hatchet. And with an "Ahah," she sees that the dream will remain just that, a dream, unless she corrects in her mind and heart the ways that keep her spirit bound.

"Oh, I am so parched and thirst dearly for water. I never knew how arid this part of the forest was. Seems odd. I will need to keep this thirst quenched if I am to continue on my journey, or I will not be able manage it. Water. I must get to water."

After a moment of silence, Thea gathers up to continue eastward in the search of water, while straight ahead flutter her trusty birds. "How is it I have become so thirsty? I am certain I know the 'High One,'" she asserts out of the blue.

The Past and Present Collide (north)

"Just who does she think she is, the little snip," mumbles a now seriously distressed Hatchet. "And that dang ungrateful bird of mine has gone off with the enemy. My father would be laughing his fool head off at me. 'How would that look, Pastoral? Can't even control a bird? The forest will fold, left in your hands. I will see to it that does not occur,'" A mocking Hatchet recites aloud rhetoric heard from the past. "Well, I will be here upon her return," he tells himself.

THE STATE OF THINGS (WEST)

Roman speaks:

"Olive, I am putting the village under your loving eye, for I am becoming heart sick with worry for Thea. I expected her return to us by now. I will ready and take my leave as the sun rises tomorrow. I trust you, Olive. Your heart is good and therefore your guiding way will be good too. May I be of any assistance to you between now and my departure?"

"There is one thing," says Olive. "As you know, there is a fox or two amongst us, and those villagers least patient are being preyed upon with promises that hold no future."

"What are these promises you know of?"

"Promises of all they desire, with no responsibility of their own. I heard them whispering."

"Oh I see. They are choosing to give up the light, that is their spirit, for a false hope. You are keen in your observations, Olive.

I suspected a secret breaking its way through the village. Remain committed to your light, with an eye on the target, and on those that will and those that won't. I will trust in the heart of the matter, with a swift return."

THE WATER FLOWS AS THE FIRE BURNS

The pine needles crunching under Thea's feet, reminding her of the thirst that calls her presence to the very moment. "Well, there will be no forgetting my assignment, I suppose one could say I am a bit controlling, but after all, I am scared for my life after all! Who wouldn't—oh, I see. So is Hatchet scared, scared for his life. Yeah, but he's much crueler. I'm not cruel, not at all," hopes Thea. "And then there is the anger and the suffering. Oh my, I have so many excuses to justify my ways, yet allow no slack for Hatchet, because he appears so much worse. I am embarrassed for myself. I am but looking into a mirror when looking at Hatchet. This is why Justice was trying to pry my eyes open, to see a truth, the awakening to who I am. I do venture there is a long way to go before my awakened state is complete, if ever. A humbling lesson it has been. I will heed silence, as my heart it seems is beginning to melt." As the silence grows deep within her, a thunderous sound ahead startles Thea to attention. She whistles in the winged ones and says:

"Before we take one more risky step into our mission, Hawk, like Lupine you need a name that announces your bravery. So here at this moment, I heartily christen you "Bravo," without fanfare but with the sincerest of gratitude for your companionship. Now, swiftly we must head into the unknown."

As this trio quickly travels down the trail, Thea readjusts her wares for comfort sake, tightens hers locks, and sings to manage her fear:

"I sing to you of something true, A peace that shan't depart, a peace that shan't depart."

As the sound grows closer, it becomes clear they must get off the path and veer south into the forest. Thea, getting anxious, slows her pace, breathes deeply, and chants:

"I can! I can! I can!"

With the birds overhead, they inch their way through the forest's thick bramble to what becomes a drop-off into a canyon of such exquisite beauty, even a doubter would realize the "High One" has been there. On the far side, lying against the canyon wall is the source of the sound that has now become a song—a glistening waterfall that reflects color as if to be a rainbow. Breathless at the sight, Thea throws out a whistle and then sits upon the ground and ponders how to safely reach the other side, speaking to Bravo and Lupine:

"It looks treacherous. You birds, I know, can get there. It is I that must get across."

The birds begin to screech and caw as if in distress. Thea shouts: "What is it Lupine?"

"Caw! Caw! Caw! Caw! Caw! Caw!"

Looking closer at Lupine, Thea notices several wing feathers missing from her right wing. Thea cries:

"Oh no. " cries Thea. "I see, Lupine. What can I do? Will you make it across? Lupine, I fear you may die trying. I will take silence for a moment, Lupine, to hear of your fate. In her silence Thea hears these words. "You live in the bitter and the sweet. That is life: bitter sweet, bitter sweet, bitter sweet." With eyes still closed, Thea says:

"I am sorry, Lupine, only the High One knows what is best for you. It is not mine to know."

THE UNEXPECTED AND THE UNKNOWN COLLIDE

Thea continues:

"Bravo, I need you to go out ahead and spot for any unexpected obstacles we may face crossing to the other side. It appears a great deal of faith is required. Otherwise I am sure to suffocate in my fear. While you are out, I will see to Lupine's well-being and map my route down into the gorge. Return safely!"

"What with water," Thea thinks, "I could easily start a fire and perform the purification ceremony that I, the forest and all its inhabitants are in dire need of. She says:

"Lupine, I do not know how to mend your wing. However, my bird, you may sit upon my shoulder and I will carry you to the other side. Your weight I can bear."

Thea skirts carefully the cliff's edge to determine the sturdiest route down a very steep incline that appears slippery and whose rock edges are so sharp they could slice the wool from its sheep without their shedding a tear. She exclaims:

"Oh my! This is why I am on this journey. It is for the treasure of life on this earth and the quality by which its people live. It is a dazzling jewel before my eyes and, yes, my heart. Its treachery a gift, for time and again it sends me into the arms of the High One, its creator. It seems the lessons I've been given are sinking in. Well, I must prepare us to take our leave."

Thea whistles in Bravo, secures Lupine on her shoulder and walks a slow wide circle, arms to the sky singing:

"The wheel of life goes round and round, and we shall not be bound."

She says:

"Okay, Bravo. As we go, tell me of your discoveries so we might avoid the harshest of conditions."

As she takes her first step into the jagged terrain, Thea realizes just how rugged the hike down will be. She also knows with a sick feeling the hardship for Lupine. "Will she make it?" Thea wonders. Suddenly, from behind her comes a ruckus—about to prove a joy long missed and forgotten. Stretching a look over the rugged cliff's edge, Thea, not believing the shining sight before her, weeps with relief:

"Oh, my friend!"

"Oh, my friend!"

They each exalt, with an embrace fit for surrender. Thea says: "Roman, Roman. whatever brought you here? LilyJack! You came on LilyJack!"

"Thea, my heart hurt at the thought of you alerting me to your distress. I felt an urgency to get to you. Olive agreed to oversee the needs of the village until my return."

"This is a moment of joy, my friend. As you can see, I have a wounded bird and we are in grave need of water. The way is treacherous at best and Bravo's job has doubled. There is so much to tell, but all in due time."

"Thea, I have a bit of water to share amongst us, but for a short we must rest if the Stallion and I are to safely cross to the other side. Meanwhile, do tell me about your journey and what service I may be while we are together. You and Lupine will ride LilyJ with me."

So Goes the Tale

As Roman listens with his entire being, Thea tells in splendid detail her adventures. She tells with anxiety of Hatchet and the trap he set and how she could not see it coming. In a soft voice she tells of Shalimar's beauty, and of Rose and Justice and their teachings. She tells sweetly of Grace and her journal, and of Grace's love with no conditions. She weeps as she tells of fear and anger and doubt. With certainty she tells of dreams and songs and dance. And finally, with reverence, she tells of the High One. She says:

"Roman, I am learning to believe in the guidance of this High One, a guidance I can rest in. Knowing now I am not alone, I am beginning to trust myself and the mission bestowed me on earth. You have heard me, Roman, and I thank you. Now let us eat and drink and rest."

One whinny out of LilyJack and the resting is over. Lupine, who has sat as still as a windless day on a low branch, is lifted onto Thea's shoulder and together they mount LilyJ's shiny coal backside as Roman whispers in the stallions ear:

"Do take care of what I love."

One whistle out to Bravo and into the unknown they point. Roman asks Thea:

"Are you comfortable?"

"In more ways than as of late. Tell me of the village and our folks. How are they holding up?"

"There are some concerns of dissension, but we are onto it and Olive is a strong young woman who will manage fine in my absence."

Shortly into the dissent the view ahead is breathtaking with its magnificent and bountiful array of colors, scents and sounds. A display that not only dances in the sunlight but if one listened close, she would hear a harmonious melody that waves through the canyon as if a symphony. Thea proclaims to Roman:

"Oh my, could anything be more lovely?"

"I think not. What a treasure amidst such treacherous landscape to travel."

Silence and awe overtake them as they follow Bravo's flight plan while keeping a steady stallion. Suddenly, Lupine falls to the ground, perishing. Thea shouts:

"Stop, Roman!"

She jumps down, kneels over Lupine and sees that she has passed. Then Thea sinks and sits for several slow moving moments....

So they go about fashioning out of leaves and vine Lupine's death dress. After tender care is taken to wrap her body in the forest's finest, the body is secured to a limb, which is then fastened to the rump of LilyJack. A solemn Thea says:

"We will say our farewells to the bird during the purification ceremony."

"Might we take silence, Thea?" suggests Roman.

"It is done."

When Thea's eyes open, they rest upon the falls she's come seeking. She cries:

"Oh, the lovely earth."

But that familiar self-doubt creeps in and the heaviness already in her heart takes on a pound. She says:

"Roman, I just don't know if I am cut out for this mission. I am certain it is beyond me. I feel strangled."

"Thea, could it be the doubt you are here to purify yourself of? I agree, with all this doubt you may not complete the mission. For the mission is to be done from spirit, not from false understandings of who you are. At the falls, during the light of day, we will make preparations for the rite of purification—to be enlivened at dusk. For now, we must whistle in Bravo."

With a shrill from Thea comes a screech from the bird. The final leg is kept in quiet, with Bravo leading the way and a resolve of surrender drifting and hovering about.

It is the roar of the falls—brilliant blue—that jangles the two back to the moment. A relief, to be sure, after so much has been endured. They dismount nearby on a moss-covered flat and take care to place Lupine's body so it will not be disturbed. They water LilyJack, feed and water themselves, then take what will prove a mystical nap.

Thea wakes to Bravo anxiously circling overhead.

"What is it Bravo?" mutters Thea. Bravo continues to fly to the north, make a dip, fly to the north, make a dip.... Then, to Thea's horror, she spies Hatchet quickly scoot from behind an outcropping of rock and then disappear. She whispers:

"Roman. Wake up, Roman. We have been followed and found."

A groggy Roman comes to attention as Thea tells of Hatchet's presence. Roman assures her:

"Well, if that's not a bee stuck in the honey jar. We will keep an eye to the sky Thea."

So the two go about collecting fallen limbs and other debris for the evening fire as Bravo keeps guard from a swaying tree branch. Small pieces of wood are whittled to burn in the fire as symbols of that which needs purifying. Gems stones are collected to remind them of the inner gifts bestowed upon them from the High One. Then, Thea says:

"Roman, let me tell of the dream I had earlier, the one Bravo woke me out of."

DREAM CONTINUED

Thea continues:

"I am here—Thea, gathering wood for the fire. You say we will need quite a bit to make it through the night. I gather stones to encircle the fire and make an honorable place for Lupine of boughs, carrying berries in remembrance of her sweetness. I then gather our whittled stick symbols of fear to be purified and the collection of gems, which be our gifts. Together we clear a path, that we might freely move around the fire pit. I am aware of being in several places at once. I am twice the observer and the preparer of the ceremony. Then, in procession arrive Grace, Rose and Justice, seating themselves upon golden thrones, which simply appear. The sky overhead, which had been brilliant with sun, is fading. You say the day is getting on and that you will prepare by cleansing at the falls. I will follow after you, I remark. While you are off, I gather berries and nuts to care for our bodies, make a prayer for Hatchet and then sing my song—

I sing to you of something true: there is a peace in all hearts

"After I cleanse, I do my hair with my finest bones and make notes in my journal of a presence I cannot name. I write that it must be the High One. I place Lupine in her final nest and it is dusk. You set the fire and a thousand birds appear, of every size and color, each perched upon a limb. Not a feather twitches. Overhead the sky stories, one billion deep, illuminate the darkening forest. The ceremony begins. First I go to Lupine's resting nest and to the chirps of a thousand birds singing her death song, present her to the fire and to ashes she returns. The wise ones sit in silence as I observe the burning of a lifetime of fears and you, Roman, of your doubts. It goes on into the wee hours until the moon wanes and the stars above seem to evaporate as the sun rises.

The birds now sleep. We bathe in the pool at the foot of the falls, call in Bravo, prepare LilyJack and begin our journey eastward to the tree house."

LOVE

"With the night bowing to the sun, the events of the evening behind will forever carry an inextinguishable spark of light. That light will be called upon to further the mission, for there is darkness ahead. The stretch to the east—the home of the sun—is also fraught with challenges that must be met with the dissolving power of the heart. For now, the morning's fragrance tastes of ginger and violets and nutmeg and hope."

Roman exclaims:

"Giddyap, LilyJ, we are head'n east!"

Thea says:

"Roman, I am restored. Last night's ceremony was a magnificent bestowing of healing. With a clearer mind and a lighter heart, I have new eyes. Do you Roman?"

"It is silent and calm in me, Thea. Thus I am reluctant to disturb the moment."

"Then I will enjoy the dew of the morning with you and the heart's memories of Lupine."

Still thoughts of Hatchet keep bursting forth, disturbing Thea's peace. "I wonder if Hatchet has returned north, or is he still shadowing us? But if last night taught me anything, it was to let go of worry and stay true to my open heart. This is a mission for Bravo," she thinks, throwing a whistle to the wind. Bravo draws in close for his instructions. Thea says: "Bravo, let us know as you soar the skies if Hatchet is shadowing us. If so, bring us to him. I wish for time with him to smooth out our rift."

So, with a lift and a screech, Bravo soars out of sight. They trot on, keeping their thoughts to themselves while basking in the warm grace of the scented forest. It becomes clear with no message from Bravo that Hatchet is no longer in their domain, and the tree house is now within sight. Out of relief for their arrival, Thea quietly thanks the High One, the wise ones and Roman. It has been the loveliest of days.

THE HEART WAKENING

LilyJack is left to graze and water, while Bravo perches atop the tree house tree to spot as eagles do. Climbing the spiral stairs to the front door of her castle, Thea comes into a very sick feeling and calls to Roman, whose curiosity had him canvassing the area, but who swiftly answers her call. She whispers:

"Roman, I sense that something is not as it ought to be and would like you to enter with me. We might not be alone."

Roman responds with a nod. Thea opens the door slowly and steps in with Roman by her side. She bellows, "Oh no!" upon noticing the disarray of all her belongings. Roman puts an arm around her shoulder to comfort, but there is more. In a far corner sits a dark figure who slowly lifts himself, then lunges toward them. They separate, causing the intruder to fall out the door, bounce off the stairs, hit a few limbs and take a hard *thud* to the ground, moaning and shouting:

"You get what you deserve!"

It is Hatchet. All the while, Roman and Thea hardly believe the fiasco. Then they head down the spiral stairs to stop Hatchet from any more destruction. Despite the bruising, he isn't sticking around for anything and limps a run and a maze through the forest, back north. Bursting with frustration, Thea drops down onto the stairs and sits with her face in the palm of her hands. She rants:

"So, being frustrated with myself is my mission, my purpose?"

Roman replies:

"There is no sense following him. He must be dealt with later. We shall collect ourselves, and I will help you reorganize your home. We will salvage that which is worthy and replace what is not with something of even greater value. Thea, I am truly sorry."

"So, might I have done something wrong?"

"No, Thea. I sense this too will prove fruitful. Clear thinking is under your doubt. Let us get about the chores."

In silence, the two return order to the disarray created by this angry-hearted man, put in Thea's path to oblige a desire of developing her highest self into being—a quest sought by those few whose time to exit the mission has passed. Thea says:

"This scene, Roman, is what I have been faced with since I arrived in the forest. You have met the enemy! The stories I could have told, you can now imagine. It seems I may be longer in arriving west than I thought."

"I don't have long before I too must return west. What do you need before I go? Would you like LilyJack, or do you prefer to journey on foot?"

"Roman, it is your blessing I wish for."

"My dear Thea, so it is for always."

Then a knock at the door comes. However when the door is opened, there stands no one. Thea says sternly:

"We are not in the mood for jokes, grandmother."

Though nothing happens, and once again Thea implores with a strong "grandmother!" No one is to be seen. Grace beckons:

"I can't make it through the closed door my dear, might you open it."

"It is open, grandmother."

"No, Thea, not that door, the one belonging to your heart."

After a long pause, Thea surrenders to her grandmother's plea and then says:

"Oh, grandmother, forgive me my roughened mood. It's just that— oh, I don't know—that I wasn't expecting to be broken into. Do come in, grandmother. Roman is here, and we could use some thought that is higher than mine at least."

"Don't be so quick and willing to shut off the light, Thea. Without the light, we are blinded and weakened. Do you understand? But let me share a story that paints a picture of what is simply the heart's nature. Roman, your presence is honored. So let us begin."

Grace continues:

"In times of ancient there lived a diamond merchant whose reputation grew vast, for he possessed the finest of facets, thus growing wealthy. But though his diamonds were brilliant, his heart was without luster. As his wealth grew, his heart dulled and he became ornery. Word of his temperament traveled—as it does— and his buyers dried up. And he became poor. As he wandered and floundered on the path of his making, a poor boy poorer than he sat crying under a tree on this particularly gloomy morning. Having noticed the elder many times before, the boy himself remained invisible. Except today, the merchant, hearing the falling tears, turned and carefully moved in the boy's direction and with a distant heart asked: 'What is it, young man.' 'Forgive me, Sire, my daily witness of your poverty overcomes my heart.' 'But you, child, have greater poverty than I.' 'Oh, but I, Sire, am rich in my Heart. My faith knows that my fate is about to change. Today, you heard your crying heart, Sire, not mine.'

"At this the merchant dropped to the ground, and where he lay an ocean grew. Having been born a fishermen's son, the boy crafted— from the tree he spent so many hours sitting under—a boat from which to fish. And word spread of the boat maker and fishermen, and he grew wealthy. He taught the poor to fish and crafted fishing boats for fishermen from faraway seas. All the while, the merchant drifted from wave to wave until, near death and in utter poverty, he was tossed ashore. The boy, now grown old, came to his aid and said: 'Sire, your stiff mind obscured your wealth. Because of you I fed the poor, and others saw with their hearts to do the same.

Many, Sire, have been lifted from their poverty of doubt. You see, merchant, your doubt was your gift. You have lived in the lap of luxury, and as a son, I now have the luxury of passing on your wealth. You see, merchant, the wealth was with your heart, but it became obscured for you. When your mind became stiff, your heart hardened, leaving those gifts of the heart buried from sight. But something greater occurred, freeing us both. So it was that freedom was being sought for the first time on earth.' 'Oh, but son, I speak to you now to leave you with this: I your father loved you enough to place you under that tree that you would have life—a life of Love.'

"Then there was silence, for the merchant had finished."

The same ancient silence hangs in the tree house for what seems a moon's phase. It goes unnoticed that Grace has taken her leave. Then Roman breaks the spell:

"Thea, Thea, Thea! This rich tale will carry you through, will it not? For I must go. My village is counting on me to lead them to what I now know is love. My heart, remember, is never far from you."

"Roman, Grace has blessed us for eternity. We must take her teaching into our bodies and into the world. It is, after all, the suffering heart that calls. I will prepare to head north, and during our separation I will meet up with you here."

Thea lays a hand on her heart.

Into the Wild Heart

For a long moment the two embrace, no need to speak. LilyJack lands a hoof to the ground with a whinny and Bravo swooshes by, fanning them with a southerly breeze, ending the moment. Roman mounts LilyJack as Bravo takes a limb, keeping an eye on Thea. Finally kisses are thrown as LilyJack turns a U and heads west, leaving Thea standing still. Meanwhile, the West Village is seething just below the surface as Olive keeps a steady gaze on the goal but is anxious for Roman's return. Ah, and Hatchet, who is now as stumped as ever with the goings on of his life, is without plan—a state he has never before found himself in.

Thea says:

"Okay, Bravo. It is you and I, Mr. Hawk. I'm to open my heart and keep it open no matter what. A tall order indeed. However, will it be?"

Thea mumbles as she heads up the spiral stairs to begin with a necessary rest, as Bravo remains perched. Thea remembers that the public library's doors are open all hours on all days. So she dresses for an unseasonably chilly day by donning her favorite sweater and hat, and heads by foot to the library. There, on the stairs she meets an old chap looking stately as usual in his suit of honor. He says:

"Hello, Ms. Thea. A pleasure to see you on this chilly day. Your presence, I am certain, will cause a joyful stir amongst the librarians."

"Thank you, Archer. It's been too long."

"Here is your key, Ms. Thea. Have an excellent read, my dear."

Archer and Thea cordially bow to one another. The she crosses the threshold into a vast and expansive hall where she is greeted by the bookkeepers, all giddy to see her. The head librarian whispers:

"You bring hope to us, Thea. Right this way. I sensed you were coming, so I laid out your books. Have an excellent read."

Thea breathes in the scents of those who have passed through this structure before her, and feels their enveloping wisdom in each breath. Spying her books on a table in the center of the great room, she floats to her seat. As she does, a most dreamy and magnificent light to read by appears to come on without assistance. The cover of each text before her bears the word "Heart." So she begins with the text in closest proximity.

Upon turning the cover, she sees the text begin to throb harmoniously as if the book itself were a living heart. At this, Thea —not wanting to do harm—closes the cover and sits back in her chair in silence, to center in dignity before resuming.

Whether one day or two—or an hour—she will never know just how much time passed. For time has mysteriously taken its leave during the complete emptying and refilling of truth and wisdom. As the beautiful light dims of its own accord, Thea closes the cover on the last volume, gathers the volumes of the Heart and is feeling for the key stowed in her pocket when the head librarian appears and—reaching for the stack of texts—whispers:

"Our lovely Thea, allow me to return the works of the Heart to your sacred space. Thea, your records are available eternally. Do not hesitate to seek here when you need guidance. You are a precious one, Thea. Remember: warm your heart as you do ours. Scurry now, the others are waiting to lift you off with their love. Oh—lest I forget, I am certain you had an excellent read!"

Before Thea can respond, there's no one in sight. So, through the grand hall and the tunnel of love she goes and then, still half asleep, descends the spiral stairs of her tree house. "It seems I slept forever," she thinks, noticing her trusted Bravo still perched and keeping watch. Thea whistles:

"Come, Bravo. I am off in search of mushrooms for my dinner."

Thea combs through the bramble for food while Bravo positions himself at the forest's edge. Soon thereafter, Thea appears with more mushrooms than a soup could ask for and, as the day is being covered with the veil of dusk, says:

"This cold north wind feels a bit like winter, Bravo."
Thea slips a hand into her pocket, and pulling out a key exclaims

"Hmmm. What's this? I don't recall having a key."

Brushing aside the question, Thea hurries back to get a fire started so to cook soup and warm the tree house.

No Measure Is There of the Heart's Wisdom

Ascending the spiral staircase, Thea decides purely out of curiosity to try the key in the door of her abode, even though it has not had a key. So, laying down all the mushrooms, Thea removes the key from her pocket, inserts it into the key slot, positions it to the left and—voila—nothing happens. Next she positions it to the right and—voila—nothing happens. Thea retrieves her mushrooms and enters, wondering where the key came from. Once inside, she busies herself with the art of soup making. While Thea dotes over the mushrooms a vaguely familiar scent wafts through the room, returning her attention to the key. She mumbles:

"Well, there's a key that seems mysterious and now a scent that comes not from my house, though I know of it. Oh jeez, could this be the work of all my busy invisible friends—well, nearly invisible. It depends on what set of eyes one is seeing with."

Thea's mind turns back to the simmering pot, which promises to satisfy the hunger inside as it warms her bones. "I sing to you of something true, a peace that shan't depart. There is a peace in all hearts, a peace in all hearts," she hums, then says:

"That's it. It all has something to do with my heart—the key, the scent, a book. I am remembering a book whose title is 'Heart Works'—no, 'Works of Heart,' that's it."

Thea lays down her spoon, wipes her hands and goes for her journal, and as she turns, there stands Rose, Justice and Grace. She asks:

"Did the High One send you?"

Grace replies:

"In a roundabout way, yes, dear one."

Rose offers:

"We knew when you remembered your book our presence would

be necessary, for this stage of your purpose is when the jewel is polished to brilliance or left dull to sparkle not in the light."

Grace chimes in: "We are the love that is sought after by all the inhabitants of earth, even Mr. Hatchet, who by the way is one of your earthly teachers, and a valuable one at that."

Justice says:

"So, might we all warm up on soup and then get about the Work of Heart? It is a magnificent library is it not, Thea?" With that, Thea's mind spins as she ladles up the simple feast. As the fire crackles in the stove, they each settle into a circle for what becomes a robust and lively lesson. Rose asks: "Thea, do you recall the library?" "I have a distant recollection, Rose." "You were there during your nap today."

"Might the key I discovered in my pocket have something to do with the library you speak of?"

Grace replies:

"I placed the key in your pocket before I left you and Roman earlier in the day. It was to keep you alert and wondering. For it is dangerous to become complacent to the spirit world. We hoped to ground in your body and memory the essence of the 'Work of Heart' and the 'excellent read' you had."

"Aha! So the scent too is from the library. Grandmother, when you said 'excellent read' I felt to weep, I am remembering..." (whispered).

Justice says:

"Your heart is the key to your life. It is a door or portal through which all is revealed. And it must remain open! Now, Thea, can you reveal to us—but think without too much effort, for it will only scramble it all up—what was revealed to you during your reading?"

"I felt being lifted out of a tightly girded box of ties and knots, then placed in a vast open field where a sea of knowing lay waiting. It was there that the lessons of my heart were placed before me on silver platters containing golden slivers of parchment. It was as if my books were places, places in my heart."

Rose encourages:

"Explain to me the places, Thea. It is crucial to use language this for the sake of clarity, as you want your blood to vibrate the wisdom in order for your feet walk in the direction your heart is pointing."

After a long pause Thea falls into sermon: "The Divine Tailwind."

The Divine Tailwind

"As if an invisible tailwind were whirling across the universe, such is the power of purpose. Infused with an organic force that propels a life along the ridges of an imperceptible cliff. Cutting away the nonsense to sculpt an existence rich with experience that takes the purposeful on a journey of inner exploration, demonstrating the courage to face the challenge meant to define the heart. Whatever it is, the individual purpose is a personal book of lessons.

"Purpose contains energy, fueling desire with such burning passion and momentum that it causes the unbeliever to believe—to believe in one's inner constitution, endurance and ability to overcome hardship while riding ever on in the tailwind. Each purpose is so rich and complex that it can and does sustain the entirety of humanity. Therefore, the focus provides acts as a compass for the quest being sought by the seeker, while ever providing purpose within purpose, revealing our unified relationship to all that is contained within the universe.

"Purpose tills us, hones us and blesses us with meaning and reason for being, delivers to us without cost an understanding of existence that reaches far beyond our grasp. It asks us to pay attention to the moment, in order that the signs be read, the unspoken heard, the unseen seen. It alerts us that we are not alone, in fact the whole universe is behind the purpose, be it true. Without our knowing, people, situations and experiences show up in lives and on paths that support and satisfy the purpose. This is synchronicity.

"One heart-driven purpose believed in can see us through years of spiritual drought. Once through that drought, we see that the tailwind, which had gone unrecognized, has been there all along— and was not only a tailwind, but a Divine tailwind at that.

"The power of purpose affords us the opportunity to walk unveiled to our full spiritual/human potential, no longer seeking outside power or recognition. For it soon becomes known, with time, that an immeasurable inner strength has lain dormant waiting for its intended receiver. It is the story of *The Wizard of Oz*. If one's purpose were in seeking courage, at some point in the journey one would reunite with the Source, that infinite and unyielding force that feeds us continuous line, equal to desire, that never leaves us and is always available. This is the power of purpose. This is the Divine tailwind.

"This wind that is the power of purpose must be grounded at the physical level in order the desired purpose and all its components and dimensions are realized in physical time. This force is what uproots that which needs transforming (false self, ego) to ensure the goal. This shift in thinking or belief equates to an elevation in consciousness, or a raising of one's frequency. Not just any purpose elicits such magnitude. The individual's purpose must be aligned and in conjoined with one's particular reason for being.

"It is prudent to be able to discern sheer mental will from Divine will—the will from which the Divine tailwind is generated. So to begin, it is the responsibility of the purposeful to know if the request to fulfill a particular purpose is heartfelt or self-will induced. Expectation of external power is a life purpose for some, with little or no regard for others and no regard for the soul's purpose.

"Purpose is the cosmic map of the universe, the map of your soul and the map of your heart. Some refer to this as a blueprint. This is the grandeur of purpose. It holds within itself the entire unseen world waiting to be called upon, harnessed and materialized for what it is—a power greater than oneself. Immeasurable potential and possibility needs only recognition and a player to step into relationship to set the momentum in motion. The desire alone to unfold the map, open the heart and own the soul will birth a life into its true and full fruition. This is the power of purpose.

"We are bathed in spheres of language, harmonies and wisdom that are just the other side of ourselves. We pay no mind, leaving our hearts troubled. We struggle, most people, with discipline because we are forcing ourselves to do things that are not in line with our true selves, and therefore we cannot for the life of us keep our energy and momentum up. We wobble like tops out of sync with the flow, rhythm and harmony of our own energy.

"When the desire to unearth the authentic self is greater than the resistance that clings to the false self, then the purpose revealed opens a spigot long shut tight, and pours forth in ebbs and flows the energy already contained but previously untapped. Required of the participant, now engaged in an ancient but unfamiliar time and space, is the willingness to bow to the wisdom of that energy, maintain an open state of being, and take up the art of no judgment. The condition we will end up in at the end of the day—or the end of our lives, whichever comes first—will reflect how each of us will choose to use our custom-ordered tailwind. So into each of our hands has been delivered some of God.

"When purpose becomes spiritual—meaning, the I desires to know who the I is in essence—remarkable things begin to occur. Dare whisper your wish to the universe and it lines up behind you and sets in motion all that a soul requires to accomplish the whispered wish. There may be one thousand steps, or there may be one step, or the last step may very well come with a last breath. The timing is not of concern, for within each moment there is reason with purpose. It is this dilemma of timing that forces the I to dig in and unearth a patience that was not there but now is, and a slightly calmer I emerges.

"Perhaps we could ponder the notion that one's purpose may be to die conscious and, to complicate the matter, that the manner and the day upon which this death will occur is also ours to determine. Most of our mortal thinking would tell us that this is absurd. However, it is not. We have more to say than we know. With this scenario in mind, the energy lines up to support the purpose and the individual whose quest this is. First to be delivered is the gift of living consciously. This is the preparation for the conscious death, for there is a listener. This begins the making of one authentic and unique individual, a process that will require a great deal of energy—or power, if you will. This power lies within the purpose and is released when and as is necessary.

"Imagine now the likes of a world whose inhabitants pursue their soul's purpose and not those of their ego. Imagine a gift of such proportion and magnitude that its power can change your world and the world. To enter into this kingdom there is but one key: know thy heart, for there awaits the Divine tailwind. Pursue the soul's purpose. There is nothing else to do."

Thea then says:

"Well, the 'places' are in the message, which once again points toward my heart and all our hearts. To help others, I must know my heart. For it is the heart's light that will set on fire all the hidden places I have yet to uncover."

Grace says:

"You have left us silent."

With slow and gracious bows, the Trio takes their leave, allowing Thea to absorb the day's lessons. Thea tosses kisses to the wind, then journals the day's events, listing by name the "places" before retiring for the night. The final sound before sleep is sweet Bravo's call.

AWAKENING

The rising sun awakens a shivering Thea, who pads across the creaking floor to heat her morning tea and warm the oven to cut a chill delivered by the moon, then pads back to refuge under the comfort of heavy quilts to sit in silence, sip her tea and offer her heart to the High One. The early hours are spent in preparation for the long journey back north to reconcile with Hatchet, for the sake of all life, a creative but oceanic task indeed.

Emerging from the warmth of her sanctuary, Thea pokes her head from the door and throws out a whistle for Bravo, who himself throws back a string of squeals. Thea chuckles and sings:

"Good morning my boy. We will be off shortly, my bird, but the last thing I must do is remove the spiral stairs to discourage possible intruders from entry into this sacred dwelling."

Inside, Thea takes one last look around, checking that all is in its proper place. She gathers up what she will need to journey, but not before adorning her hair with feathers and bones while twice laying a hand on her journal to assure herself of its presence. Thea says:

"Now where is the key?"

"The key lies within, Thea."

"It is under my pillow grandmother."

Thea smiles, and Grace says:

"I had to see you off to wish you well, my sweet dear. You are shining like never before. You shall be easy to spot."

"Oh, grandmother, your love fills my heart. It has erased my doubts and has blazed into my innermost self the origins of my new well-being. I hope my gratitude pleases you. I will know you are with me."

Thea descends the stairs and then manages to tuck them out of sight. She puts her eyes on Bravo and turns north.

THE WORD IN MOTION

The wind coming out of the north is a bit brisk and busy and is met not with favor by Thea, who, just beginning, is more than a touch bothered. She says:

"Already I must remember myself and all I have been given. Even to accept this bothersome wind and its story. I am seeing that the invisible world wants to be made visible."

"I must put into practice my lessons," Thea thinks.

WALLS GO UP—WALLS COME DOWN

Bang! Bang! Bang! Hatchet hollers: "Ouch! $%#@#$!" Charleston offers: "Let me help you. I am experienced, having constructed many of the dwellings in the West Village." "Had you not come to see things my way, I might find myself in another bramble. This wall will see to it that we are not at the mercy of that girl." "I worry not of her, Sir. Besides, the others will be here before the moon's light." "What numbers might they becoming in?" "It is hard to say. Less than a dozen, but more than sufficient for the mission."

"Aren't we all on a mission?" Charleston keeps the thought to himself, grimaces and says:
"Worry not, Sir. Your security is assured."

"I will rest the leg I sprained in the fall, while you gather more logs. It is all her fault."

Charleston pays no mind, for his only interest is finding the stock-pile of gems that were long ago dug up and removed from the West Village. He knows this gold mine will bring him and his band of troops their freedom. He says:

"Ah yes, yes, yes, happy to be of service."

So the clanging and the pounding and the cussing drones on with barely a word between them. The day wears long and the wind comes as the sun closes its eyes. Hatchet announces:

"Nearly finished and my security will be secured."

"Concern yourself no longer, Sir. Just a few more logs, materials for latches and your freedom is sealed, and I am off to canvas for the final provisions."
"Then a fire must be lit, for the cold is settling in and a rough night it will be without one."

Looking around, Hatchet realizes he is speaking to no one, so limps off mumbling about the cold and the fire. It isn't long after that the fire is roaring and Charleston's overdue return is beginning to cause Hatchet to itch. Suddenly unexpected guests seem to be arriving—with a boldness about them—into the compound. Aroused by the ruckus and in combative mode, Hatchet grabs up a crude weapon of sorts and snipes out in a menacing voice: "Who is trespassing on my property? Name yourselves."

"We come from the West. We come in peace, we come in unity of your cause, we come with battle in our bloods. My name is Gretian."

Relaxing the joint-crushing grip on his weapon, Hatchet, silent for a moment, moves closer to the direction of the voice and thinks, "Just how much trouble can a girl be?" He says:

"Might there already be one of you amongst me?"

Stepping into view, Gretian speaks:

"Yes, Sir. That would be Charleston, our master."

As they approach, the light from the fire reveals three other young men with statures of strength. One of the young men reaches out a hand and says:
"You must be Hatchet. It is our pleasure, as we were not privileged a personal introduction on your past visits to the West Village."

"Yes...and you are?"

"Let me introduce us. Well, as is clear, this is Gretian (nodding to his right). This here is River on my left, and to his left is Andrew. I, Sir, am Ledger. We are here to handle for you any threats the girl Thea may attempt to bring upon you. Just where might our Master Charleston be?"

"Well, he could be lost by now. He went for supplies some time ago and seems to have disappeared."

Just then, a shout "Hello!" comes from behind the newly erected fortress. It's Charleston.

"Hello, my friends. Glad to see of your arrival. I have been out gathering and got myself turned around. How were your travels? My dear Gretian, it is good to see you...."

A semi-irritated Hatchet cuts in, prodding Charleston about his supply venture and—more precisely—the time lost:

"So was it the fading day that caused your disorientation, or are there ghouls out there in that there part of the forest?"

"Oh so sorry, Sir, to bring worry to you. You've been through enough. I simply lost my sure-footed self I assure you, but I assume you properly met my friends, did you not?"

"Yes, and the sooner we get a plan, the happier I will be."

Then Ledger asks:

"Might I respectfully request that us weary travelers first get some grub—our bodies are famished—and then a good night's sleep?"

Lighting the Dark

So it was decided to end the day around a cauldron of soup, a warm fire, and an explosive silence. However in the middle of the night, another conversation, another plan, another war was being carved out of greed. Charleston says:

"We must keep our voices down. I will not risk the fortune about to be placed in the palms of our hands. We are so close to freedom. Our mission can be accomplished in no more than two days.

Should Thea arrive before that, we will act in disguise of our intention just as we are doing with this foolish man."

River says:

"Master, tell us what you discovered tonight."

"Well, I can't be certain—the light was not good—but I do think I was onto an old foot path now camouflaged with the brush of the forest. It leads to what appears to be a cave of boulders where a treasure of gems could easily be stowed away. I will send Andrew and River out at dawn with a rough map of the trails to scout. I will tell the fool you are to spy on Thea, and the rest of us will plan the second war."

Gretian whispers:

"What is my role here, Charleston?"

Charleston whispers back:

"Keep the guy charmed and feeling cared about—that is a good question—and Ledger will act as my backup as River and Andrew carry out the task of unearthing our cache. Then all of us will take on Thea. A ruse unprecedented in the history of this forest!"

Then sleep calls them.

While they are sleeping, Thea, who's found shelter near an outcropping of moss-covered castle rock, is in full regalia and preparing to mount a peace offering to Hatchet, something truly unprecedented in the history of this forest. Then something quite unexpected occurs, and then another something of equal surprise.

As Thea dances in the dim moonlight, singing up a sweat, from her fingertips drips the doubt that must not and cannot go with her north. She says:

"Bravo, I am so happy to see your return. Where have you been, my friend?"

Bravo flaps with vigor, screeching and swooping near Thea's aura with an excitement that causes her to wonder what Bravo has seen.
Thea says softly:

"Bravo, I need you to sit on a limb overhead, keeping a hawk's eye out while I sit under the tree in an act of silence so better to listen and receive any ground vibration moving in our direction."

So the silence hums, and Bravo moves not a feather, but not for long. When Thea lays an ear to the ground to better judge the pulse shimmering through her body, she hears a floating voice not hers say:

"A bud is about to blossom."

Without holding her breath, Thea waits as a ground rumble approaches in inches—its speed so slow she begins a silent chant to maintain her concentration that she not be run over by fear and lose the wise instruction from inside her. As the vibration draws closer, Thea grows calmer and inquisitive. "I wonder," she thinks, "what prattle is happening here in this forest tonight."

Suddenly the gentle rumble ceases, and out of the shadows a sight more fragrant than a bouquet plucked after a morning dew moves toward her gallantly—Roman. Thea weeps. An embrace brings down a shooting star of mystical proportions, then comes a bitty snort the stomp of a right hoof—Lilyjack too desires nestling, and with sweet delight, Thea meets the wish. Then she says: "Roman, whatever brings you to me in the middle of an unsavory forest night?"

"I come with a warning. We moved as snails through the forest this night so as not to be seen or heard. First, let us see to a small fire out of the wind. We can tuck in near the rock and I will unpack the provisions I bring you."

"Well, let us be quick. I am anxious to hear the story you bring. How is the West doing?"

"While some parts have come into balance, other parts have not. That is what brings me here."

Before continuing their conversation, the two settle in for the long night. Then Roman says:

"I remind you of the brewing dissension that was left in Olive's care. It appeared to have calmed down as I departed. This, however, was an illusion being fed to us—one that, yes, even I partook of."

"Are Olive and the others in danger?"

"Your question brings me to why I have come to you. Those leading the dissension have moved north we believe and are possibly at Hatchet's awaiting your arrival. Not for your benefit, Thea, but to shore up Hatchet's agenda."

"Oh my. So will you be joining me then, Roman?"

"Well, that is only part of it, Thea. There is more to tell. It appears that the visit to Hatchet is suspect and nothing more than a ruse. Their true intention is to convince the old guy that your mission is without scruples, while behind his back they are seeking the gems stolen from our village."

"Roman, tell me—these characters, who are they?"

"The leader of them is Charleston—that would be Master Charleston—Ledger, River, Andrew and, sadly, Gretian. It seems each is under their master's spell."   .

"What spell might that be? Let me answer my own question. Is it the spell that carries a hint of truth—the spell of convincing lies, like sugar on spoiled cake? Is it the spell that charms fear, like shiny foil that enwraps deadly candy for a baby? Is it that spell, Roman?"

"It is that spell, my Thea."

A somber silence sits with them now as the seriousness of the crime infiltrates into the very blood that beats through their hearts. A daunting task indeed. Then Roman says:

"But there is more. The light that you call forth is with you, Thea. It brought the winds so you would have to shelter down at this particular outcropping of rock. When the Hatchet family dug up the gems from the West Village, it is here where they buried them. You were brought here to protect the gems from being heisted again!"

"Is this why you have come, Roman?"

"Yes. Together we will unearth the stones, and LillyJ and I will pack them back to the West where they belong. The stealing must end. The risk for you is steep, these gems are wanted by hands that heed no law. Our determination must be greater, yet wrapped in truth."

"I am beyond words. I will let the magic of the mystery settle in my bones. Roman, you have not answered. Will you go north with me?"

"No, dear one, this is your fishing trip. I have been counseled. Trust your fate and your destiny. You will not be left alone. Olive will meet you there. She is strong, and in observing your way she will be mentored by you. For her seeking is genuine."

Roman puts Thea's hands in his. She says:

"I see. And who is your counsel?"

"It is Justice."

"With that I must not argue."

Thea nods. So the fire that is waning is reignited to warm them as they rest through the rest of the dark period of the day. The plans go forward, the digging and the packing begin, and decisions by the minute are made. Thea's solution agenda is formed with clarity, certainty and strength grounded in trust of the High One. Roman will make several night runs to the west—the cache is mountainous as it is luminous. Thea will review her night in the library. She is certain it holds the secrets she must carry with her.

Blinding Is the Veil of Deception

Charleston says to River and Andrew:

"Keep your voices down! We must not appear suspect of any suspicious behavior. Please look like you are getting along—now what is it?"

River replies with hostility: "We found no tantalizing sign of suspicious hideouts, Sir. We think, Sir, you are mistaken."

"It is not your authority to question me, now, is it? I suggest that both of you create a charade to spend the day away in search of those gems that are going to mean your freedom, understood? Well, I see everyone is up and around. Let us plan our day. The plan goes like this: Gretian and Ledger will win over the heart and mind of Hatchet. River and Andrew will continue their search for the stolen and hidden gems, while Master Charleston continues constructing his game of webs. As for Hatchet—he is keeping guard."

River says to Andrew:

"Let us hit the trail."

"I am right behind you."

So down the trail they head, when out of the blue a flock of birds mysteriously appears overhead, having arrived from no apparent direction. Andrew asks River:

"Well, what do we make of this?"

"I say we had better recite our 'Code of Control' aloud with gusto."

Each with their head to the sky, the code begins to tumble out of their mouths as if a battle cry:

> *Our mind is our weapon Our determination is our eternal power Our will is ours to will our desires Our goal is ours alone to drive out opposition Our purpose is ours to collect in abundance,*

wealth Our plan is our method of maintaining control Our final
act is our freedom rooted in our ideology only Great be our minds

River says:

"They are maintaining their position overhead. I think they might be trying to lead us to the gem stash. I say we follow their lead."

Off the beaten trail they go and are soon quite turned around, as one can get in a forest. The birds stop in midair, and the two miners drop their wares and begin digging on the spot. The spot relinquishes nothing more than soil on soil.

Andrew says:

"This smells of a sour soup—aha! Oh my, look!"

He points to where the birds are now standing. It appears to be a burial mound. River laughs:

"I'd say the sour soup is fermenting sweet. Let us shoo away the birds and get to digging. This is going to impress our master."

Then a diabolical thought comes upon Andrew, whose scratchy mood could use a buffing. Excitedly he says:

"We could take the stash and move to high ground."

"Hmm, that is odd. The birds have vanished, it seems, in the same mysterious manner they appeared."

The two begin a digging that continues until exhaustion puts them to sleep.

Pacing his fortress, Hatchet is exhibiting signs of frustration with the newcomers. Tension is steaming off of Charleston.

Gretian calls: "Hatchet, let us cook a feast for our impending freedom celebration. Ledger can snare us up some rabbits to slow roast as you and our master make final war plans. I sense the trappings will soon explode, But with our determination, the fight will be short." Before Hatchet has even a thought, Charleston moves all the pawns into position. He says: "Yes, Sir Hatchet, I agree. Gretian's plan sounds solid as gold. Gretian will clean the place and steam the trappings for what Ledger hunts up, while you and I roll in to guard the final boulders. It is certain to be a sweet sunny day." Then River and Andrew return from scouting the enemy and announce: "We are all on our way to paradise." Charleston chimes in: "Great be our minds." Then an eerie shadow appears. All eyes are raised to the sky, where a silent and still flock of birds rest. Hatchet shrieks:

"This, remember, is my fortress. It looks like things are beginning to get odd. That girl is up to something." Charleston responds: "Might you be overestimating her? Her ingenuity is not, I am certain, what you believe it to be." "Do not underestimate me either."

"Oh, let's not get the war started yet. We are here, after all, to make your life gentler."

The big, smiling master throws his arm around the old man, but Hatchet pulls away. In a most ungracious quiet, each goes about the prescribed agenda as the still birds stare down on them. But by the time Ledger goes off to hunt, both have fallen fast asleep.

Last Load

Roman says:

"I will return the final load of gems to the west after dusk, and in two days time Olive will meet you on the south end of the north camp. Will you be all right, Thea?"

"Your presence and its kindness have strengthened me, Roman. I will stay strong in spirit."

Bravo suddenly lands hard on the ground, screeching a hawk's screech with feathers puffing up, and lifts to the nearest branch and stares straight into Thea's eyes as if delivering an announcement from some ancient monarchy.

Thea prods:

"Whatever is it, my little bird?"

Bravo closes his eyes and then opens his eyes and then closes his eyes and then opens his eyes, staring into Thea's eyes. Roman exclaims:

"Thea! He is dusting them with sleeping powder. It is an ancient warring technique used to divert the enemy's attention while a peaceful reconciliation can be forged between leaders. Bravo has prepared a way for you, Thea, and eased my heart as I leave you to return west."

"My incantations to the High One provided the portal for an answer that existed before there was [a question]. But, my dear Roman, I must—before you take leave—speak aloud a truth that must be spoke. You love me?"

"I do love you. You love me?"

"I do love you."

The two stand before each other, passing the love declared through their eyes. Each knows the trueness of the soul they each gaze into. No more is said.

Mounting LilyJack and pulling the reigns westward, Roman hands a white velvet bag down to Thea where she stands. Then he departs. Having now honored a vow taken long ago, their destiny lies clear before them. Drawing open the bag, Thea's hand lifts out seven exquisite gems, each a luminous color found only in the sky or maybe the ocean or maybe a rose garden. Grace pops in to say:

"Well, well. The two of you over joy me."

"Oh, grandmother, my perennial doubt is once again denied me. What better gift could befall one such as I am?"

"Well, granddaughter, are you going to smother the joy or let it sing? I can't hold my breath any longer."

"Where do I put it all—the joy—it is a fireworks going off in me and will for eternity."

"I won't keep you, my darling, I know you have a peace war to wage, but I wanted to be the first to kiss the love lit upon the two of you. I am off."

VISIONS OF INSPIRATION

"I am called now to purpose, which I will enter with a glad heart and a replenished well of inner strength, knowing the dusting will wear off before the mission's completion," thinks Thea.

Theeeeeeeeeeee-aaaaa Theeeeeeeeeeee-aaaaa Theeeeeeeeeeee-aaaaa

Thea declares:

"I am being called. From inside me this voice is rising. Is it the High One, I wonder! Bravo, we must get on north."

Theeeeeeeeeeee-aaaaa

"There it is again, my name being sounded out as a chant. Hmm, is it my Soul? My gosh I believe it is. Listen. That's it. Listen, my Soul is taking up a grander space to greater guide the battle of Heart-over-Might."

Taking out the white velvet bag, Thea again pours forth into the palm of her hand the brilliant gems, now aglow, and ceremoniously and with great care joins them together and secures them around her neck to remember the love and truth tour she is on. Then she says resoundingly:

"Okay, Bravo. Finally we are off."

Theeeeeeeeeeee-aaaaa

"I will take the short cut north to avoid all the boulders we encountered on the first trip," thinks Thea.

Theeeeeeeeeeee-aaaa

Thea sighs:

"Hmmm..."

Silence, Silence, Silence

An eerie and mysterious void comes over Thea. As it does, there is nothing on earth to be heard, not even herself. A most unusual event. Then a rain of monsoonal proportions arrives, then stops. And the sun comes out.

Thea sighs:

"Wow. I will keep silence."

"Oh! I see, I have a purpose though I am not the purpose," humbly admits Thea to herself. "So what am I?" comes an almost imperceptible thought. Grace jingles:

"Hello! Hello! Hello! It is us, your favorite trio. We've come to keep you company and see to it you stray not from point and get lost in your mind."

Thea, remaining silent, ignores the three and carries on till Bravo alerts her to the simultaneous arrival of every creature in the forest, all lending a graceful bow to Thea as she approaches the trail least traveled by humans (its surface as ancient as time). Even the turtle bows, if you can imagine it, and the elk and the possum and the wolf—it's like a holiday parade. When it is over, each howls or screeches or bellows or sings in its respective voice with indescribable melody. Thea says: "Bravo, my bones are vibrating with the sight and sound that this forest sweetly offered up for the mission ahead. Odd to say but I feel holy, Bravo! I guess, like the Trio, each is sending us off into the ascent of another way: truth and love."

So, down that ancient trail, like waves they roll, Bravo overhead and a singing and praying and chanting Thea moving ever so briskly through what she now knows to be an enchanted forest.

She worries out loud:

"I must be sure-footed and graceful as the deer to not show late for Olive's arrival north. Do I have a plan in place? And just what is it I am going to say to bring about desire enough to turn a stuck and gruff old hoot of a fellow such as Hatchet to seeing things with new eyes?"

From off the trail, and leaning cockily into an elm about to fall, Ledger speaks:

"I hardly believe there is a conversation to master an inspiration such as yours, dear lady."

Thea speaks calmly:

"My, my. Your appearance unlikely—I am Thea by the way—wonders in me your purpose for being out here in such a wilderness?"

"Well, I woke from a sleep deep in the forest and my companion, I fear, has perished. We came to do some mining and seem to have gotten turned around and could use some help. And what speech are you about to give? To whom, dear lady?"

"My name is Thea, please, and might it be that a perished friend be of greater concern than my speech. By the way, did you arrive from the West Village or do you know of it?"

"Our companions are in the North Village."

"More importantly, how can I and my bird assist?"
Thea is changing the subject when Bravo flies by in a tippy low sweep. And like the tipping Elm, the fellow with the perished friend tips to the ground as Bravo rises again as if a genie rising out of his bottle. Thea says:

"Bravo! My dear Bravo, it is the sleeping dust is it not? I feel the trio nudging me. We will make haste."

Hmmm, there are others," Thea thinks. "I will converse with the High One regarding my approach with Hatchet and peacemaking for the west."

THE REHEARSAL

Thea says:

"'Dear Pastoral Langely, I have been sent by messenger to advise you....' Oh jeez, I can't say that. I'll try this: 'Hatchet, there's a war going on and I am here to end it.' Oh no, none of this sounds right. Okay, what about this: 'Hatchet, let me reintroduce myself.

I am Thea, Thea of the east, and I arrive here, this moment in time, having been graciously entrusted with a mission whose message of life wrapped in love, coddled in truth and emanating hope, will once again bring the forest and all of its dwellers to balance, harmony and abundant life. The forest and our people are in need of your goodness if we are to restore and regenerate the life entrusted to our care. Our well-being and yours are at risk of critical decline and death by neglect. We do not wish for you to do without, but instead wish to respect your life and ask that you too would respect ours. We will never agree to be your enemy, though we know there are a few amongst us who are against all of us. Unless their hearts and minds are turned, they will be strongly encouraged to leave the forest. We know the High One is with us to see to an outcome that is correct for all of life. Might you please consider?

Lest I forget: Meet Olive. She is my apprentice learning the art of peaceful negotiation. If you need anything, she will assist you. Your needs are of concern to us. Now, the others, I sense, are soon to wake. Mr. Pastoral Langely, I believe you to be a kind hearted soul. Should you join in this quest, your burdens will be lifted and many a heart will be lightened. I need you today.'"

"It seems a convincing plea to me," thinks Thea. Then she hears Justice speak:

"Don't count your flowers before they bloom."

"Justice, what are you saying?"

"Just that, Thea."

Then all went silent. Then a gallop and a gallop and a gallop. Thea calls out in a tender whisper:

"Oh my, is that the sound of hooves I hear? LilyJack, is that you? Olive?"

Into view the chariot and the apprentice emerge, and Olive cries out:

"It is, Thea. It is us."

"Shhh, we mustn't be too loud lest we are discovered. It is so good to see you both. Come, Olive, here off the trail so to keep LilyJ from view. We will speak of what may lie ahead of us and how Bravo is assisting the mission. A warning comes from Justice to not count our flowers before they bloom."

Instantly, a chill courses through Thea and Olive, making it hard to speak and leaving them feeling lost as if walking through a bog, as if something or someone were shaking everything upside down, as if they were being tossed high into the air, as if it were all about to end.

An Unexpected Descent

They both struggle to speak. Olive whispers:

"What is this we have been wrapped up in, Thea?"

"I can't be sure. Let us not get shook up. I will speak to the High One. Join me in silence, Olive, for guidance and the courage to walk into the unknown. The goodness has an existing route. We must follow it and change our idea a bit. Just as I suspected, the energy following the defectors from the west has got to us. They are trying to stop us. Olive, do you believe in this mission and its wisdom?"

"I do, Thea."

"Then we shall continue forward, and each difficult step we land on the ground will release us from this force we have been wrapped in, and therefore we will arrive in full strength to the north. Let us rest a bit, let us eat, let us ready LilyJack, let us then head in."

A resolved Thea thinks, "The deeper the dive, the greater the ascent."

SOUNDS AND SIGHTS AND SERVANTS AND SLAVES

"Pears, Olive. We need to serve up a feast of pear dishes—each bearing a spice, an herb and a flower that will go down gently—to disrupt those wretched and famished who wish to do us harm. And I know just where to get them. I will send you on with LilyJack. You will head straight south through the Valley of Sound. It is the ancient route to the gardens of Shalimar. No need to go farther. All you need will be found in the valley. There you will receive a word. That word, Olive, is our solution and the pear is a carrier. You must also bring a collection of seeds and nuts, and fallen bark on which to serve this meal. Then come straight to the North camp. That is where you will find me."

"Thea, why is it called the Valley of Sound?"

"When life here was a vibrant and pulsing force, the sight of the inhabitants was honed to precision. Upon their realizing that all colors—from the dullest to the brightest hues—existed in this corridor alone, the inhabitants curiously began to hear a sound. Soon this sound became an elixir, and the gardens grew lush and the folks effortlessly carried that sound in them and lived. Sight and sound spiraled up and up and up, sending shivers in the North dwellers. Then the spiral down began. That, Olive, is the short version. We must hurry now to tend to the need placed at our feet."

"So, Thea, was it the truth they were hearing?"

"Later, Olive. We must move."

"How was it, Thea, you came upon this solution?"

"A dream, Olive. It was a dream. Now shoo! Bravo will see to you."

THE HERALDING

So the two depart, each in her respective direction. Meanwhile the heat for first place builds in the North Village, it is parting the clouds above. Thea will have her hands full, but full of what? Before she rushes north, however, she rummages through her belongings, unearthing the very thing needed for this sort of battle—the golden shoes left by her bedside the morning after her excursion to the library. Booted and ready, she is off.

A smug Hatchet says:

"My, my! Look at what the wind blew in—the girl. So what trouble are you dragging behind you onto my hearth this round? Because it will be a round of pure malice, I warn you. Tell me now just how might that fancy you, girl."

Thea replies calmly:

"If it minds you not, may I address you as Pastoral Langely? That is your knighted name, am I not correct? Before you answer, I am here to visit upon your guests from the West Village. They are here, are they not? It has been a distance between our last eyes upon each other, and so I am jumping in my heart to get a view and speak a word and discover what inspirations have traveled them in this direction. So, dragging no trouble unless perhaps you are hiding some, Pastoral Langely."

"What is there to hide? From whom would there be a reason?"

"I happened to meet up with a young man from the West Village. His name is Ledger. Has he been here?"

"Yes, he passed through."

"Of what did he inquire? Was he alone? Pastoral, I am here to wash clean the troubles between us and the west, and I need your help.

From the looks of things, it seems you have company."

Suddenly from all four points of the earth, standing erect as soldiers stand Charleston, Ledger, River and—as if the eye has been tricked—Gretian. Then Charleston, speaking in a booming voice, begins heralding edicts right and left:

"Gretian, position yourself by Thea instantly. Ledger, gather up all weapons and bring them to me. River, secure the barriers around the perimeter so our guest thinks not of escape without peril. Hatchet, ready yourself to secure with assistance the North camp."

Silence. Thea's eyes had never left her feet while the orders were flying. Words from her books are beaming into her heart and mind from the golden boots now illuminated. After a deep breath, she raises her head and says:

"I am Thea, and I have something to say: this mindset that you have has, for too long, done too much harm. Harm me if you wish. There is something a new afoot, and you will not prevail for long."

Charleston chides:

"Oh, Thea, you are a fool of folly if you believe your own words."

Silence. Raising again her head from the light emanating off the golden boots, Thea speaks:

"I arrive with a new law, are you listening? It is the law of union. We will be what we do to others because we each come from the High One. My sight reveals to me that we are united as if one continuous thread, and to this understanding we are being asked to return."

Shuffling nervously at his end of the world, Charleston booms a ridiculing snarl at Thea and claims: "Before the moon can rise and set, we will have what we want and you and your law will be on your way."

Thea directs her full gaze and stance toward Charleston and says: " What do you want?" Hatchet barks at Thea: "They have come to see to it that I maintain full control of this forest that you, girl, invaded." She says: "So, my sight tells me the precious gems from the earth have something to do with this. Is that not true Charleston—excuse me, Master Charleston—meant no disrespect."

Charleston retorts: "Well, Thea, your sight is quite right. We are guarding them so they do not fall into the wrong hands, as they are the sovereign property of the Hatchet family."

"Might the wrong hands be yours, Master Charleston? Or did my sight suddenly go wrong?" At this, Gretian and the others begin to appear nervous. Hatchet snaps:

"So just what is the girl implying, Charleston?"

Charleston jolts back:

"I suggest we follow through with orders and end this silly discussion. Whatever music you hear, Thea, isn't meant for any of our ears, and we have heard enough. So folks, let us continue on our journey!"

An eerie feeling descends over the camp, nothing moves, not even a branch or a feather. Breathing is halted. Time appears to stand still. Overhead, the birds with the sleeping potion have swarmed to the rescue. Only three are left awake: Thea, Gretian and Hatchet. Thea asks:

"Before the others awaken, who would like to tell me what's really going on here."

Hatchet shouts:

"It is just like you heard, protecting my forest and gems from the west. They offered their help because the west is no longer their cup of tea."

"Is that true, Gretian?"

Gretian timidly replies:

"Why yes, Thea, it is true."

Thea casts a glance toward Charleston and says:

"So, Gretian, are you under his spell too? I sense I am not being told the truth and we are losing time, the sleep the others are under is going to wear off. Gretian, I have a strong hunch it is you who is holding out and it is unlike you to be without the beat of your own heart. You know it's key to everything, so might you brave to utter the truth before the party stirs?"

"Oh, Thea! I have been blind with desperation for calm and peace. The village and its disarray churned our hearts distraught. And yes, vulnerable I sought solace from Charleston, who planned to masquerade as Hatchet's army only to unearth and confiscate the gems, then flee from the forest. I sold my heart, Thea, for riches. You Hatchet, you were about to be betrayed."

Thea says: "So, Pastoral Langely, we were both about to be betrayed by my people, who chose a destructive course and attempted to turn your game on you, do you see?" Hatchet exclaims: "I will decide who I am going to trust, if any of you." Thea says: "Our time is running out and we have to make a new plan. Who is with me?" Gretian smiles and says: "I am with you." Hatchet says: "I stand alone." [Then he falls asleep.]

A New Arrangement

Thea says to Gretian:

"With Hatchet now asleep we can create a map to guide the

mission's intention: to solve the unbalanced harmonies amongst the forest and its dwellers. Gretian, our sight must maintain a pure focus. It will guide the creating of the plan and assure no harm is done. Perhaps you might gather the materials necessary to fashion each of us—that is you and I and Olive—swords."

"Swords!?"

"Yes, Gretian, swords to remember that though we are women we are strong on the inside, and it is that strength we will call upon to meet the day. We will also need seven goblets for the pear juice."

Thea bows. "Oh my," thinks Gretian on her way, "swords and goblets." Meanwhile Thea seeks a bit of solitude to silence herself. Grace whispers:

"My dear sweet granddaughter. We have come, my dear, for it is lesson time."

"Oh, grandmother, I should have known the High One would not leave me to struggle alone."

Rose explains:

"Thea—Justice and I too are with you, and we must get started. Time is running out."

Justice asks:

"Do you have a question for us, Thea?"

"Yes! What do I do?"

Grace says:

"Well, first silence your heart and mind, then Justice will begin, my child."

Justice says:

"I will speak to your competence and your strength, Thea. You must guard against ordinary thinking, thinking that is too small. Fearful thoughts limit the High One's grace—the pouring forth of the way of the heart, where original notions bring about harmony and the truth your mission is seeking. Do you understand, Thea."

"Yes, Sir, I think so."

"Beware not to give way to demands that carry a threat. They serve only a few and solve nothing. You must be prepared to trust and follow your inner knowing, though it appears uncommon and nonsensical. Allow no other to swipe at your wisdom or to question your sanity. You are not loco. Be very wary of black and white options. For only the truth can open the doors and the windows, allowing the light to shine on innumerable creative and joy-filled solutions. Listen to your opponents, then speak kindly to that which lies under the surface. Most importantly, speak with certainty, a firm resolve and always with your heart. Hearts melt walls. And lastly, Thea, your practice speech will serve only if your eyes are clear to whom you speak. With every breath, breathe in the High One. If it is any consolation, we are with you."

Rose says:

"Thea, the victory is performing the mission that abides in the soul of your heart. That is all there is to do, goodbye for now."

Grace says:

"Good bye, little love."

Thea says:

"Thank you, grandmother."

Then sighs:

"Oh my, trust is no easy task. However, I must trust. Gretian, come. Let us sit a moment as I map out a plan.... We will let them carry on with their intention, observing closely Hatchet. By then, Olive will be here. But not until it becomes overly fired up will we go into action. Follow my lead. You will know when I bow my head for a significant amount of time. Upon my looking up, prepare to come to my side. At which time, I will reveal in a calm tone Charleston's true intention. It will get nasty. Trust me, Gretian, Charleston will attempt to send the fear of life through you. Stand strong in the truth and follow my lead. They will wake soon and not remember having been put to sleep. The lapse in time will go unnoticed. So, let us get about our preparations so we are energized for the coming experience. May the High One reign over all of us, truly."

Charleston, with a smug grin, says to Thea:

"So, I can't imagine what possible threat you are expecting to shake us up with that would alter our business here. Like you, we are also on a mission. It is to save the reigning north empire, whose roots are deep into this Hatchet clan. Try uprooting that history! River, Ledger, how are things? Might we need a private meeting? Gretian, keep an eye on the girl."

Thea feels the boots illuminate and hears a reading of sorts that goes as such:

> Be present, here in time you are strong
>
> Be focused, then your words will not falter
>
> Be divine in spirit, sing the melody heard
>
> Be brave, whilst you shudder and fall
>
> Be humble, it's your portal to ancient truth
>
> Be fueled by fires of eternal love and live

Then she describes a vision:

"Well, it appears I am peeking through an empty kaleidoscope. Where, I do wonder, did its colorful animation go? Hmmm. Perplexed I feel. It is revealing what is missing, and what is missing is the holiness that once imbued their vessels—bodies, that is—and the holiness has been replaced with a space unattended, becoming a darkened cellar for fear, loneliness, greed, control, coldheartedness, a warring spirit and serious isolation from eternal truths floating freely in the pulse of the universe. This anxious scramble to claim what does not belong to them is an illusion of survival and incomplete understanding of reality. I am viewing the roots of troubles. Ah, reason for hope is what I see. I see each distrusts the other, equal to who they claim is the enemy. This is quite a vulnerable situation to find oneself in. They would die to this terror and exaggerated belief for safety that rings of no truth whatever, a virtual wasteland. The crime of humanity is humanity on humanity. This vision is hardly lovely, and harder still to swallow that illusions are a way of life.

So, telling the truth gets tricky. It is something most are unfamiliar with—the truth. Imagine being asked to alter the ground you have stood on for many an existence. I now know my enemy, it is a falsehood that spans the globe. A firm but gentle motion is required. I see they are tying tighter knots in the weave to secure during opposition, as to maintain control and not unravel the flawed but familiar design. Cutting through the denial will require a finesse of balance that comes only from a higher order of justice."
"Whew, that was fascinating. I must prepare to take action,"

thinks Thea, looking to the sky where Bravo is hovering. Thea says:

"Bravo! Sweet bird, I am so happy for your return. And where might our Olive be?"

Then a faint whinny is heard, and the sight of Olive brings relief to Thea's heart. After bows and hugs and greetings of kisses, and a nuzzle for Lilyjack, the pears and nuts and stories are exchanged and the two young women set about—with Gretian—to decorate and advise and cook up a cooperative strategy of high justice for a high-stress situation shown through the vision to be deteriorating quickly.

Thea says:

"They will wake to a banquet and festive climate, catching them a bit joyfully off guard, and then glance around, notice that the trees are beginning to sway and that atop each is a bird of a different feather. Together, the birds will provide an enchanted symphony to hold the atmosphere in check when things heat up."

Olive asks:

"Might this gala of a war have something to do with the word I received from the High One while collecting pears, Thea?"

"The word, Olive?"

"The word is 'wonder,' Thea. It is to keep the heart young and open, and the mind supple and open, and the body vibrant and open."

"Yes! what a lovely word, Olive. Do you see now, Gretian? We are not alone. There is guidance all around that is for the well-being of each of us, not just a few."

Gretian says:

"I am beginning to see. I will trust it in time."

Swiftly the swords are carved, the goblets retrieved and polished, the pear tarts and pie and broth readied, the nuts and greens displayed, and a long table of downed ancient tree stumps set for a holiday. Bravo orchestrates the symphony. Without noticing they have slept, all gather at the table, taking without direction their respective seats. It is wonder in the making. A rather grumpy Hatchet speaks first:

"Another girl. Now who are you?"

Before Olive can even open her mouth, Charleston breaks in:

"It is mighty fine to see you again, Olive. Silly to have not guessed an entourage from the West would arrive to save sweet Thea and the day. I suppose Roman will be next to buckle up and join in the fight."

Olive gestures in Hatchet's direction and says calmly:

"Yes, my name is Olive. No, Master Charleston, we do not believe Roman's presence is demanded."

Hatchet eyes Thea and barks:

"Well, let's get on with it."

As Thea's golden boots begin chatting up a storm, and as the trees gently sway to the rhythm of the birds' melodious hum, Thea rises from her chair, turns to Hatchet and begins:

"Sir Pastoral Langely, I want you to know that in my heart I am deeply sorry that your Lupine passed on while in my care. I recognize her companionship was all that was left you upon the tragic demise of your entire family. I would, sir, treasure your forgiveness might that be given. Your life's hardship I share, having lost my parents as a younger women. A tough road, to be sure. As the garden has bloomed again in my life, I know it can in yours too."

Thea raises her goblet to Hatchet and recites an ancient, sacred song known to heal the heart. Charleston, chuckling at what he deems to be a spectacle, says:

"This is about the gems and who reigns in this forest. We are here to see to it that it remains as is, in the hands of Sir Langely, to whom you refer. We remain put until we find them and deliver them into those hands."

The others look down while gobbling up each scrumptious pear dish. Olive whispers to Gretian:

"Do you know, the pear's juice softens the perception."

Charleston, who is not eating, continues to wrangle. Thea asks:

"Whatever brought you here, Charleston?"

"The west has grown greedy, and many of us were weary of the disgruntled attitudes displayed by yourself and King Roman. We desired to be of help where help was needed, to answer a call, you might say..."

Before the uneasy Charleston has finished, Hatchet butts in:

"So, where are my gems?"

Thea says:

"The gems, sirs, are the property of the land in the west. It is their point of origin, purposed for the fair trade of the four corners of the forest, to be dispensed of properly and justly. They were not meant for the sole ownership of any of us, but instead were to be dispensed of wisely. This forest is suffering in all of its corners, and life must be restored before it is too late to undo the harm done. Done, I must say, from harmful hearts."

Charleston, rising from his seat, begins to circle the table and insist that Hatchet deliver a precise point of search because time is up, when Hatchet says to him:

"Are you threatening me?"

The intense circling continues and no answer comes. Ledger and River rather shyly join in circling behind Charleston. Gretian eyes the swords. Hatchet is up and standing at attention. Olive retrieves the swords while gesturing to Bravo to continue his orchestration. Thea, left sitting, feels her golden boots heating up and from her inner world hears softly an instruction: "Tell where the gems are."

Thea stands and speaks:

"The precious gems have been returned to their home of origin. Roman and I, under the light cast by the moon and the peace the night brings, back yonder a bit, secretly secured the transfer."

Slamming his now fisted hands on the table, knocking several goblets to the ground, a very steamed Charleston bulges his eyes at Thea and stammers and spits before he can speak a sentence. Hatchet nearly faints, is now on his feet, sits down, stands up again, sits down again and finally stands with both hands gripping the table's edge to steady himself.

Charleston says:

"Ledger and River, prepare. Gretian, get ready to put that sword to use. Whoever made you Queen Thea, Thea? You have put this forest in peril and crippled the one who could save it."

A now less aggressive River and Ledger circle the camp. Gretian positions herself and her sword between Hatchet and Thea but brings no attention to her new alliance. Olive stands as erect and steady as Thea, as Charleston's level of excitement escalates to near terror. But there is more to be revealed. Bravely stepping forward, Thea begins:

"Perhaps, Charleston, your outrage is twofold. You may take your leave of the forest now and be on your own, or make a clean sweep of the cobwebs that have grown over your heart, causing a blindness of sorts. This choice is yours. Will it be peace or no peace?"

Out of the blue, Gretian, staring directly into Charleston's eyes, speaks:

"You lied to Mr. Langely, and so did I and River and Ledger. Pretending to befriend and help Mr. Langely save his power over the forest, we came here to locate, dig up and steal away all the gems for our own pleasure. But it was you who wanted all the power. I regret going along with the scheme, and I apologize to you, Mr. Langely, for pretending to be something I was not."

The Turning

Before the sky can lose a drop of water, Hatchet and Charleston are on each other, rolling on the ground as the punches fly. Bravo and the birds come to help, the trees stop swaying, LilyJ reels on her hind legs and whinnies, River and Ledger attempt to break up the fight and the Trio approaches Thea, when suddenly something eerie occurs. The ruckus stops. Charleston stands up, brushes off the dirt, turns and runs from the forest as Hatchet lies there as still as death. Everyone's breath stops. Thea kneels down beside Pastoral Langely as the others gather round in silence and the Trio, with the High One's help, speaks words of wonder while Thea's hands breathe enough life back into Hatchet to determine that an attack of the heart has occurred. The imminence of the situation is glaring. The trees begin swaying in solemnity and the chorus of birds reply with a somber chant, while the others tend to Hatchet. But somewhere in the fray, Ledger disappears.

Thea speaks softly:

"We cannot worry after Charleston and Ledger. We must make a bed of healing boughs of pine and flower blossoms from off the forest floor, we need your help, River, to move Pastoral once the bed is prepared. Please, someone bring me a goblet of pear nectar."

Earnestly and silently, like worker bees they prepare the bed and, with a device rigged up by River, Pastoral is eased onto his healing bed to heal. Hours pass as the others softly sing Thea's tune:

There is a peace in all hearts!   There is a peace in all hearts!

The Trio remains on site, infused with the High One's breath. At dawn the next day, Pastoral stirs from his bed, restored with a new heart and vision.

The Return Home

With Charleston and Ledger having taken flight from the forest, moving forward with Thea's mission should flow with ease—or so it is thought. Something no one has suspected is to be discovered, and the final move homeward will carry a new weight of unprecedented proportions on their shoulders and in their hearts.

Thea says:

"Let us pack up LilyJack with the least necessary of our provisions and head her west with a note to Roman announcing our plans to be home very soon. And, Pastoral, we will leave River to tend to you till you are fully recovered—at which time you are welcomed to return west with him and perhaps forge a new creation between our relations with each other and the forest."

River says:

"Before we head out, I will do a sweep of the area. There might be signs of our comrades or the direction they took flight."

Once again, Thea's golden boots begin to emanate a light indicating a message coming forth. Thea, with eyes closed and mind silenced, begins to feel within her heart a troubling score of energies that cause her to tremble. An ill feeling falls upon her. Opening her eyes, she sees River moving swiftly toward her. With breath labored, he chokes out his findings:

"He is dead, Thea. I found Charleston and he is dead."

"I am speechless. One of us has fallen hard, and his death and his life were of great value if we simply look closely into them. We will honor this life as the High One would. We will send him off in beauty. Are you all right, River? I feel you are best suited for giving Gretian the news. I will speak right now to Olive and Hatchet, and then we will begin our preparations. First I wish you to take me to him."

At the body, Thea ponders aloud:

"It appears a death by the natural causes, by great stress. Like, perhaps, his heart gave out. There are no outward signs of a struggle, so it's most certainly inward."

River says:

"That is my hunch too, Thea. Yet I am very concerned about Ledger and his whereabouts, and his knowledge of this startling situation."

"We shall signal our souls to seek for Ledger, inviting him to rejoin us if he would."

Thea turns north and adds that she will seek silence, as burial preparations are under way.

The Ultimate Lesson

Turning away, Thea cries. Her tears flow as if they will never cease. Finding a tree to rest her back against, she takes out her journal and writes:

Dear mom and dad, I no longer know, and my lessons it seems are failing me or I them. I am weary in my blood. This path I have chosen is about killing me, and I in my foolishness thought I was on the path of life and love. I yearn to hear you. They say we are not alone, but oh, try to convince this orphan. I need hands to lift me up, mama and papa.

Grace sweetly whispers:

"Thea, Thea, Thea. It is I, Grace."

"Oh, grandmother, I am so, so tired."

"We know, dear, we are listening. We have come for your last lesson. We are sorry for all the sorrow. Your joy is drawing near. Take several deep breaths, Thea, to relax. It will help for the spirit of the word to sink deep into your beautiful mind and your most lovely soul."

Rose says:

"You are being purified, my dear, We smile at your weariness for it opens the door of surrender to the High One, the source of your being. And with surrender comes a vibrant energy that feeds to you the wisdom your path requires. Surrender's companion is letting go, perhaps the toughest of tests. Letting go of all the ways that life isn't what one believed or hoped. Illusion weakens one, Thea. The truth makes strong. Now you are positioned to release the inner obstacles of battle and struggle against the way life is. Acceptance. Acceptance, Thea, opens up the world of Choice and will. What will you make of yours, Thea? Remember, dear one, you are destined to return to whence you came. In so doing, you remember who you are. To align your choice and will with the High One is wise. What you are experiencing is a 'livingship,' which is a relationship infused with life and light and love. This ship will carry you through all waters, truly."

Justice says:

"Thea, your inner tenderness is your outer strength. With that you face your daily challenges. Often return to the well that is your heart. There, you will bring yourself to full restoration. You will always be learning that what you have received on this leg of your journey is a foundation born of truth, which you must continue to seek with a humble heart and hand."

Grace says:

"Sweet Thea, the lesson has ended. Rose and Justice will part with a blessing. I will be by you eternally. One last bit: your mother and father will come at your request; you only need to ask. I love you, my sweet one."

"I love you too, grandmother."

An Honoring

Rising up from the ground, Thea goes to Olive and Gretian to check upon their well-being regarding Charleston's death, then on to Hatchet to see about his health and how he is taking the news. The women then join River, who is tending to the business of the burial and ceremony. It will be a long day with the birds overhead swaying in the trees and Bravo bird-chanting from his perch over Charleston's body. An eerie and solemn humming takes over as preparations are put in place for the final farewell.

River turns to Thea and says:

The pine needles, rose petals, buds from various flowers and trees, water to be blessed, rich soil, a feather offered up by each bird, a prayer written by Gretian and a gem from the West Village— an offering by Hatchet—are put in place. Charleston's body is cleansed and wrapped and ready to be placed into the earth, its mother, while freeing his spirit back to the High One, our source."

Thea replies:

"Let us tenderly raise this man and gently release his body into his final bed of rest, letting our hearts sing off this life, knowing it is before each of us to forgive and see him with the greater eyes that, because of him, we now have. Our new eyes will forever be his gift to each of us."

Silence falls upon the scene, heads are bowed, and gently the silence gives way to song and chant and wishes as each slowly moves around the sacred space, tossing in the rich soil sure to produce new life. The celebration ends with a crackle off the forest floor in the distance. The birds turn and all eyes are on Ledger, who is propping up Hatchet with his makeshift walking stick. Slowly they move toward the grave site. Their presence is warming as the procession around the grave site resumes for a final blessing.

Toward Dusk

Ledger says:

"I left out of fear, in search of Charleston, but could not find him. Then I heard a horrible scream, but by the time I got to him he had passed. Again I decided to run, thinking I would never return. It was my belief that my part in the gem scheme might not be forgivable. I did not have the courage to look into your eyes without shame. I apologize for myself."

Thea says:

"We all carry a smudge in us that needs polishing, Ledger. Your returning was courageous. Let no one sit in judgment. It is much wiser to be humble than think oneself above another."

River says:

"We need you, Ledger. Our hearts are heavy enough with this loss and the betrayal we had set in motion. Our blame must end here."

Thea says:

"Olive and Gretian and I shall leave at dawn with the sun shining upon us. It is energy we will need. For I see that fatigue and weariness is settling into our bones. Who will stay with Pastoral?"

Thea turns to River, who says:

"I can. Ledger, will you accompany the women back west?"

"Yes, yes I will."

Thea says:

"Pastoral, when you are strong enough on your own, we wish you to join River upon his return home, and there we can forge a new relationship with each other and the forest. We ask your forgiveness for what has occurred here. We wish to lay down our swords, bow to the goodness in you and offer to you our hearts, our hands, our clear minds. Your acceptance would be a gift of grace to each and every one of us. Pastoral, please ponder our humble invitation."

Turning from Pastoral, Thea announces her need to get rest for the long walk home and her intention to walk it in silence. At which point, the camp fire is put to an ember. The sobering and somber veil of the day settles like dust, leaving an indelible imprint on each witness. It is an end.

Dawn

With a pin-yellow horizon at their backs and a great silence around them, Ledger and Olive and Gretian and Thea move west to Shayba village.

> *Light I have a life to live I have a purpose I have all I need When I listen I feel a movement I feel a guidance I feel a higher idea When I open I can do what is asked I can face fate and destiny I can be truly alive*
>
> *When I hear I will learn love I will bend to love's will I will be love, love*
>
> *When I believe I speak the truth I speak with my voice I speak: action silence word*
>
> *When I look I am I see a vessel I am I see a carrier I am I see a creator When I trust I know source intimately I know I have a part I know I am not alone When I listen*
>
> *When I am still the High One is revealed*

In the meantime, LilyJack has returned to Shayba alerting Roman that in short time Thea and the others will return. This means a celebration—in place of hardship—is what answers the hopes and wishes of all the villagers as Roman announces to prepare for the coming of Thea.

At the Gate

Ledger, speaking to both Olive and Gretian, says:

"Ahead of us there looks to be a resting place where we can drink and eat and rest until Thea catches up. What do you say?"

Gretian says:

"Yes."

Olive says:

"Yes."

The snapping and crackle of the forest floor alerts them of Thea's approach. She gestures to the others and says tenderly:

"As I walk in silence, the lessons taught, the experience in the forest and the magnificent dreams had are weaving their beautiful tale inside my very being. My heart, it seems, has expanded, and so my mind. It is an interesting and lovely happening. I, it seems, am more I."

Olive says:

"Will you continue to mentor myself and the others?"

"I will do all that is asked of me. It is what we all must do, just what is asked of us."

Thea adds:

"I will retreat again until our arrival at the gate of Shayba."

In short time, greetings are heard echoing through the forest. For it seems the entire village is at the gate, each with a grand welcome on their face.

Roman's voice comes:

"You have returned."

Soon there are cheers and tears and so much chattering and rambling, nothing much can be understood. When the noise calms and the tears end, Ledger, Olive and Gretian pass through the gate to the village's center to begin the storytelling. Roman stands sentinel-like at the gate for Thea. Bravo perches upon the limb of a nearby tree. Then LilyJack shows up with a whinny. Upon first sight, Roman cries:

"Thea!"

Thea, now running, cries:

"Roman!" Reaching for Roman she whispers: "I am here." Roman whispers: "You are here." He folds her into him for the rest of time, eventually passing through the gate to begin life with eyes brilliant with light.

EPILOGUE

" Love is the only engine of survival..."
—*L. Cohen*

So the storytelling went on till into the wee hours, and not until everyone's voice was heard and everyone's need was addressed did the fire go out. The glow of that fire, even after all these years, still hovers, as if a halo.

River returned along with Pastoral, who never fully recovered physically, but oh how his spirit did soar, becoming Shayba and the forest's most devoted advocate. His physical transition from this world to beyond came but one year later. Bitter/sweet it was: bitter because we grew to love Hatchet, sweet because he left with an open heart.

With a renewed cooperative community, the forest became well managed and restored itself over the years. Shalimar blooms as if tropical. Its waters sparkle. The gems belonging to Shayba are reestablished to their original purpose: to sustain the life of the forest and its inhabitants. If we listen closely, they speak to us of their gifts. Skald, the village I came from, is a bustling hub of artisans. I visit there often and sleep in my old tree house. Shadows in the North is now alive and industrious.

Olive has grown into a majestic and wise woman who is still guiding and teaching all those who seek the wise path to travel upon. There are many of them today, for which we are grateful.

After finding the peace that was missing for each of them, Gretian and River married and raised three boys to be strong and kind. They are satisfied and giving Souls.

Ledger studied the ways of wisdom with Roman and spends his time traveling and teaching around the world. His personal act of forgiveness transformed and opened his eyes from a narrow to an expansive view of life.

LilyJack and Bravo aged and passed, as we all will, but for now their offspring keep us young.

The Trio for eternity will visit. My time with them is of great comfort, their teachings invaluable. I love them so.

Roman and I have aged together, our bond inexplicable, our love eternal. Our marriage took place eons ago.

I, Thea, learned: the High One, simply put, is the High One.

About the Author

Colleen Brezny brings forth ancient teachings, eternal truths and perennial wisdom necessary to spiritual development and transformation. Educated in the philosophies of all spiritual and religious traditions Colleen teaches and guides the seeker searching to understand our truest and most authentic nature, that which breathes in us and around us. This wisdom, a sacred magic, answers and softens the heartbreak that is inevitable, leaving behind the gift of inner freedom and profound knowing.